Maurice
and His
Dictionary
A True Story

Written by
Cary Fagan

Illustrated by
Enzo Lord Mariano

Owlkids Books

For the family – C.F.

To the families who are obligated to flee their country, still today – E.L.M.

Acknowledgments

I want to thank Amy Tompkins for finding the perfect home for the story of my father. It was Karen Li's inspired suggestion to use the graphic novel form; for that, and for her wonderfully sensitive editing, I am very grateful. Thanks to everyone at Owlkids Books. My brother Lawrence provided the family photographs at the back. And a thank-you to Diana Cooper-Clark. A much earlier version of the text appeared in Taddle Creek.

Owlkids Books acknowledges the financial support of the Canada Council for the Arts, the Ontario Arts Council, the Government of Canada through the Canada Book Fund (CBF) and the Government of Ontario through the Ontario Creates Book Initiative for our publishing activities.

Published in Canada by
Owlkids Books Inc.
1 Eglinton Avenue East
Toronto, ON M4P 3A1

Published in the US by
Owlkids Books Inc.
1700 Fourth Street
Berkeley, CA 94710

Library and Archives Canada Cataloguing in Publication

Title: Maurice and his dictionary : a true story / written by Cary Fagan ; illustrated by Enzo Lord Mariano.

Names: Fagan, Cary, author. | Enzo, 1996- illustrator.

Identifiers: Canadiana 20190232129 | ISBN 9781771473231 (hardcover)

Subjects: LCSH: Fagan, Maurice, -2017—Comic books, strips, etc. | LCSH: Fagan, Maurice, -2017—Juvenile literature. | LCSH: Holocaust survivors—Belgium—Biography—Comic books, strips, etc. | LCSH: Holocaust survivors—Belgium—Biography—Juvenile literature. | LCSH: Holocaust survivors—Canada—Biography—Comic books, strips, etc. | LCSH: Holocaust survivors—Canada—Biography—Juvenile literature. | LCSH: Lawyers—Canada—Biography—Comic books, strips, etc. | LCSH: Lawyers—Canada—Biography—Juvenile literature. | LCGFT: Nonfiction comics. | LCGFT: Biographical comics.

Classification: LCC D804.196.F34 F34 2020 | DDC j940.53/18092—dc23

Library of Congress Control Number: 2019956184

Edited by Karen Li
Designed by Claudia Dávila

Manufactured in Guangdong Province, Dongguan City, China, in April 2020, by Toppan Leefung Packaging & Printing (Dongguan) Co., Ltd.
Job #BAYDC73

A B C D E F

ONTARIO ARTS COUNCIL
CONSEIL DES ARTS DE L'ONTARIO
an Ontario government agency
un organisme du gouvernement de l'Ontario

Canada Council for the Arts
Conseil des Arts du Canada

Canada

Publisher of Chirp, Chickadee and OWL
www.owlkidsbooks.com

Owlkids Books is a division of bayard canada

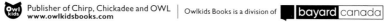

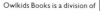

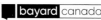

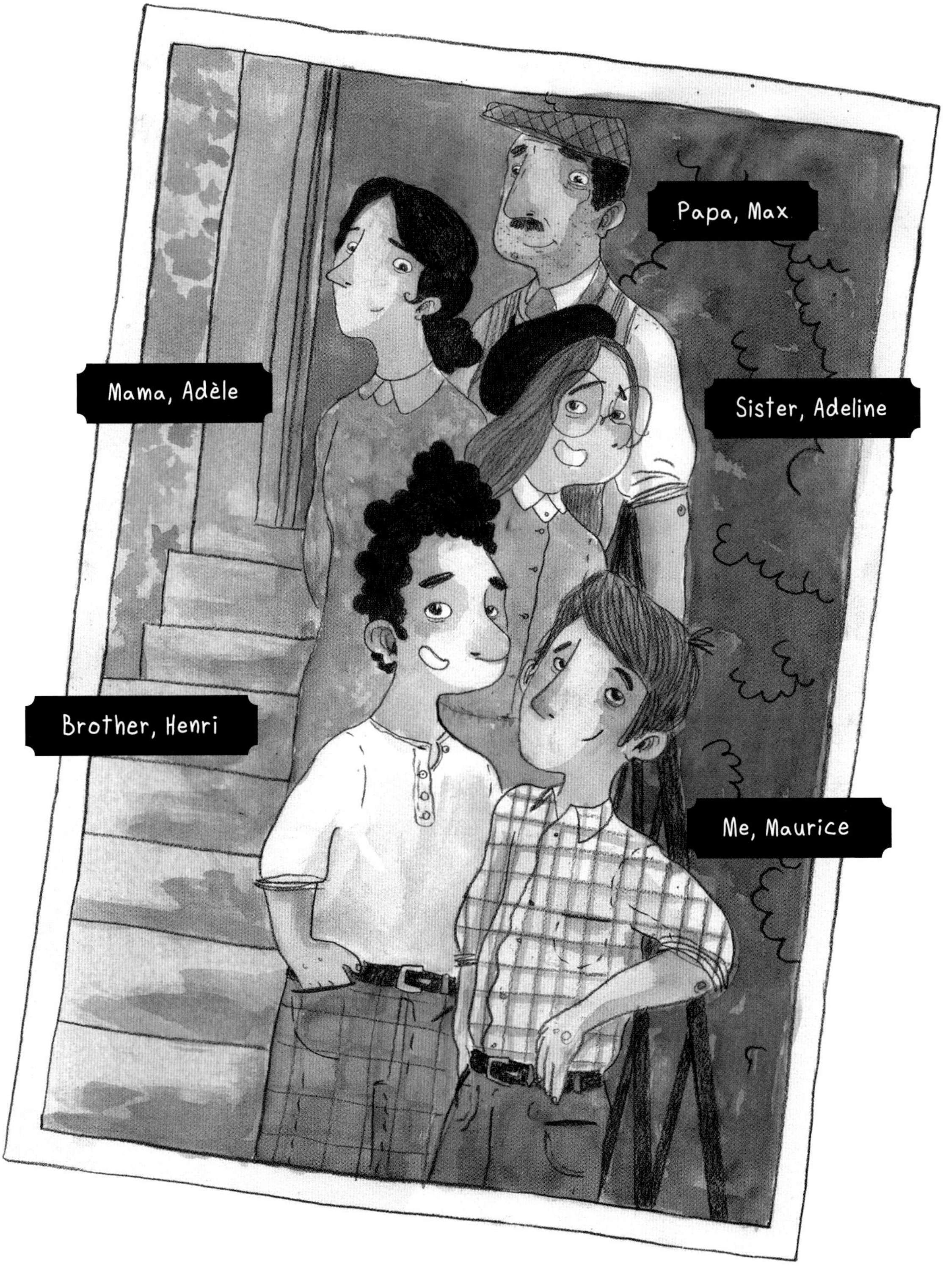
Papa, Max
Mama, Adèle
Sister, Adeline
Brother, Henri
Me, Maurice

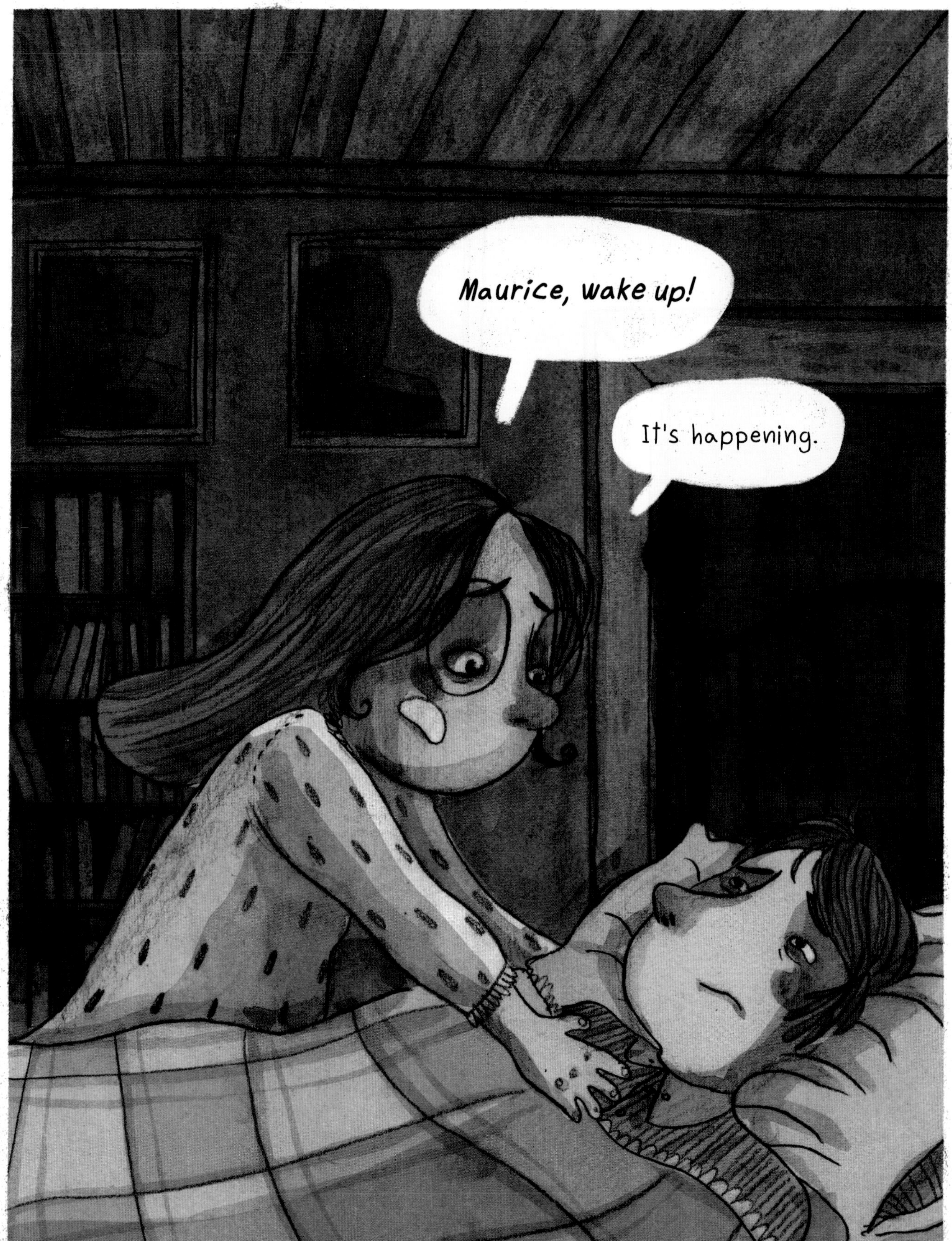
Maurice, wake up!
It's happening.

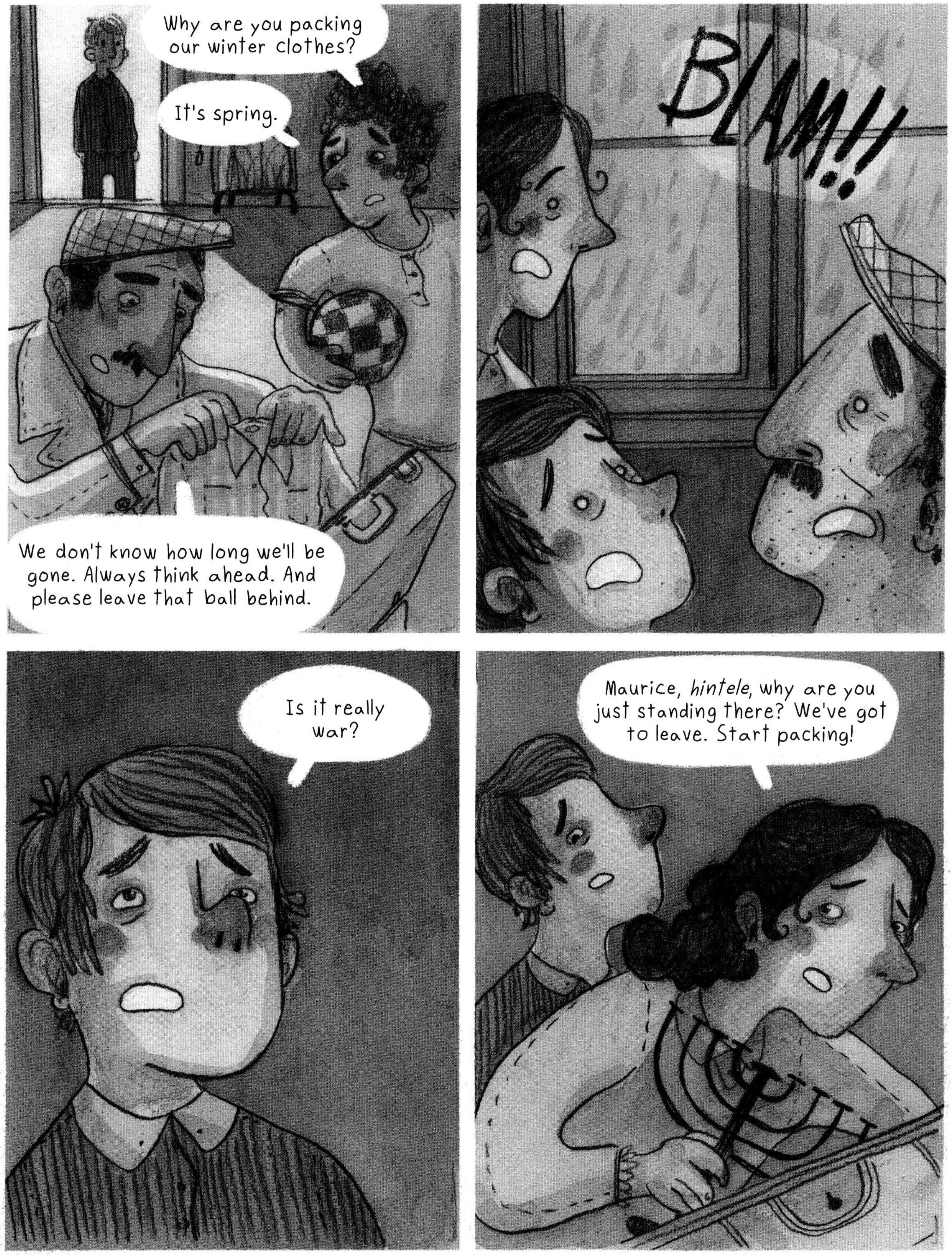
Why are you packing our winter clothes?
It's spring.
We don't know how long we'll be gone. Always think ahead. And please leave that ball behind.
BLAM!!
Is it really war?
Maurice, *hintele*, why are you just standing there? We've got to leave. Start packing!

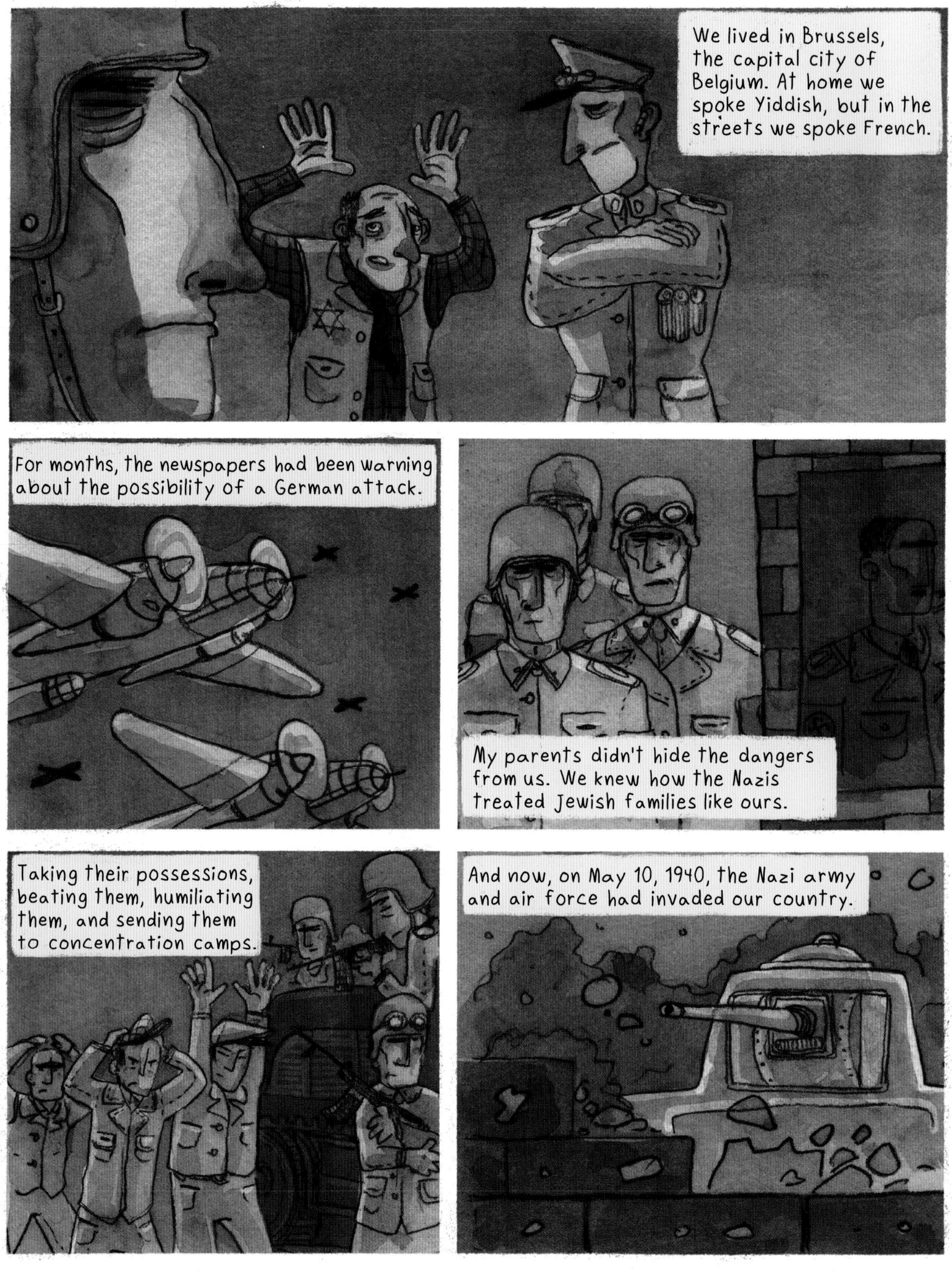
We lived in Brussels, the capital city of Belgium. At home we spoke Yiddish, but in the streets we spoke French.
For months, the newspapers had been warning about the possibility of a German attack.
My parents didn't hide the dangers from us. We knew how the Nazis treated Jewish families like ours.
Taking their possessions, beating them, humiliating them, and sending them to concentration camps.
And now, on May 10, 1940, the Nazi army and air force had invaded our country.

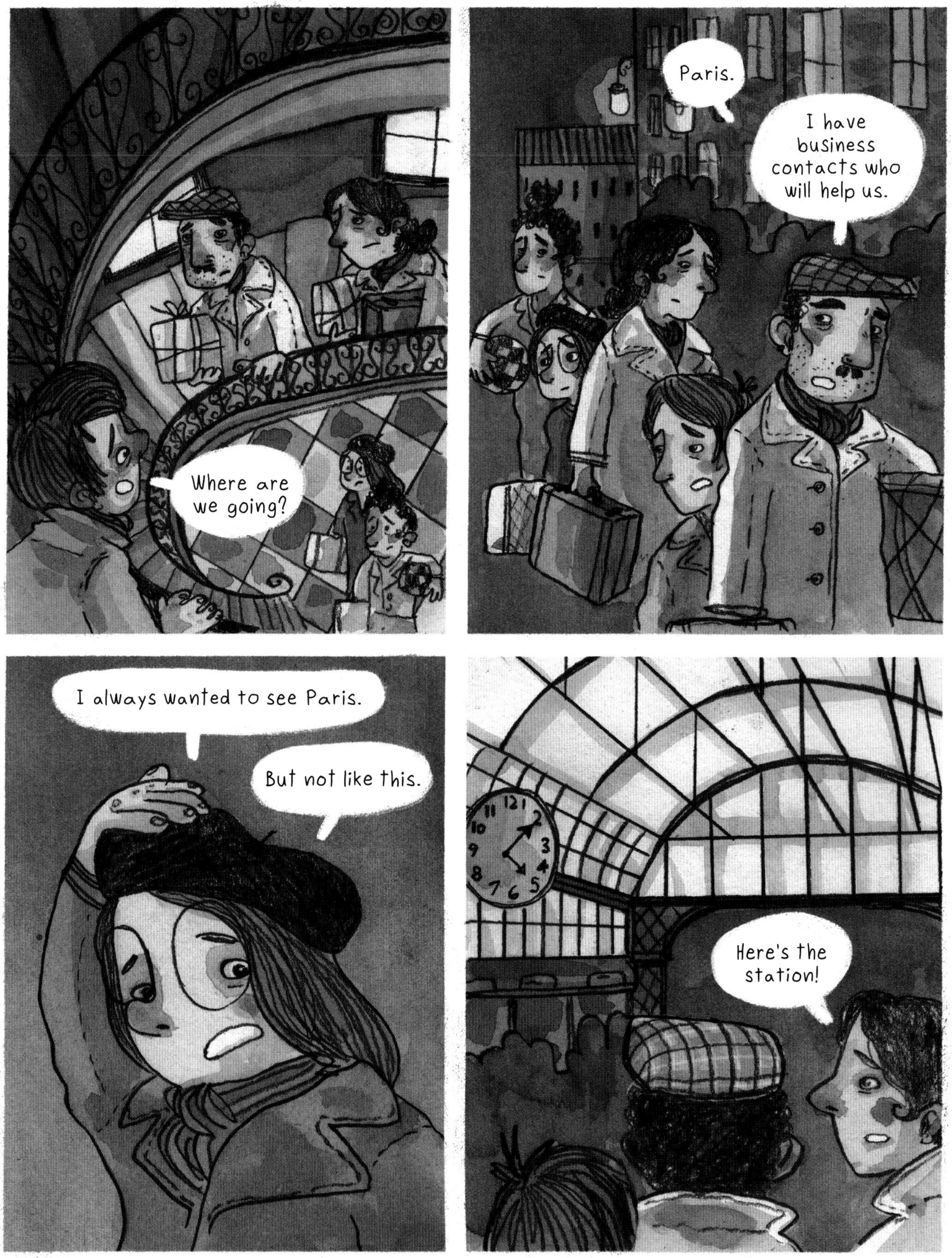
Where are we going?
Paris.
I have business contacts who will help us.
I always wanted to see Paris.
But not like this.
Here's the station!

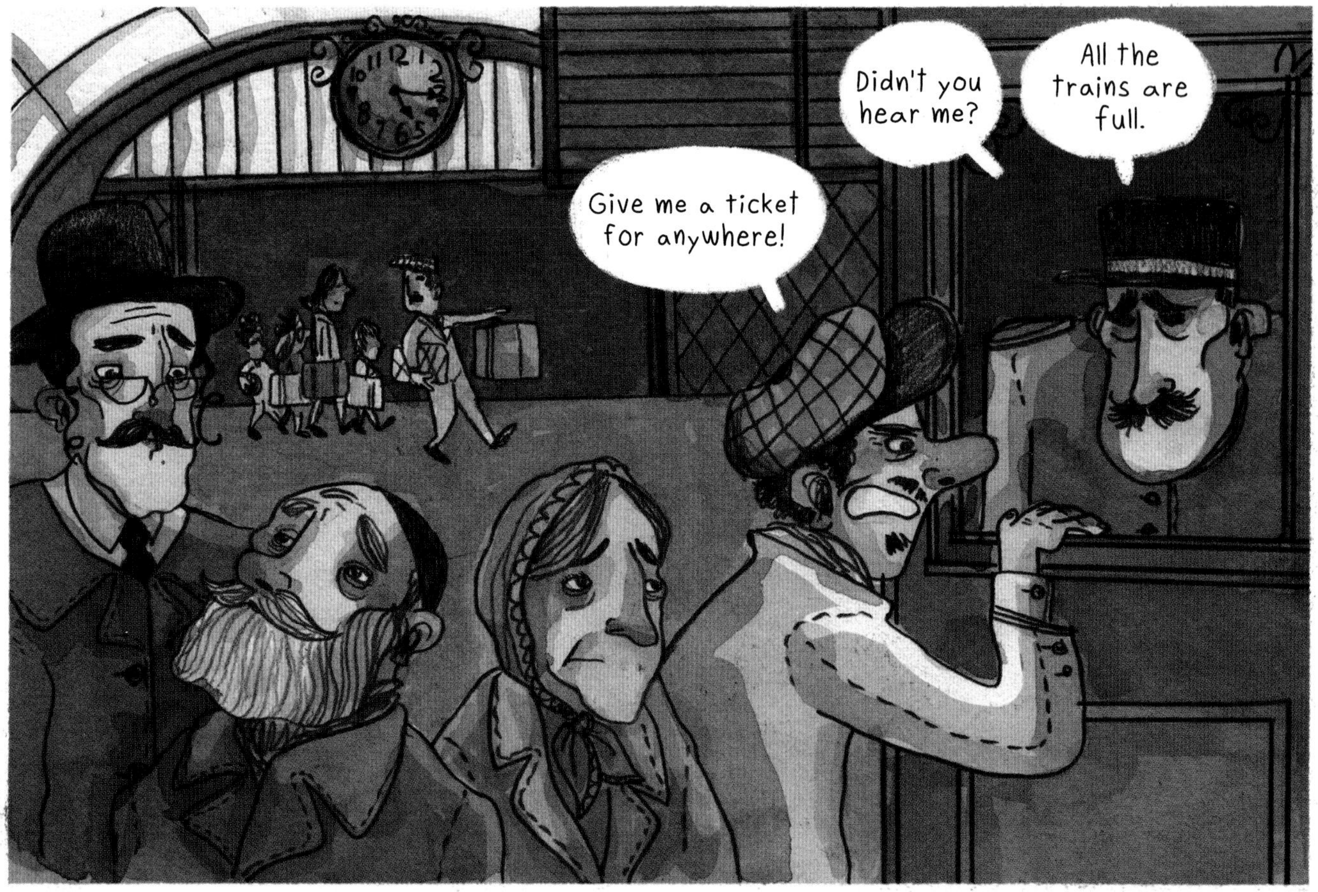
Give me a ticket for anywhere!
Didn't you hear me?
All the trains are full.

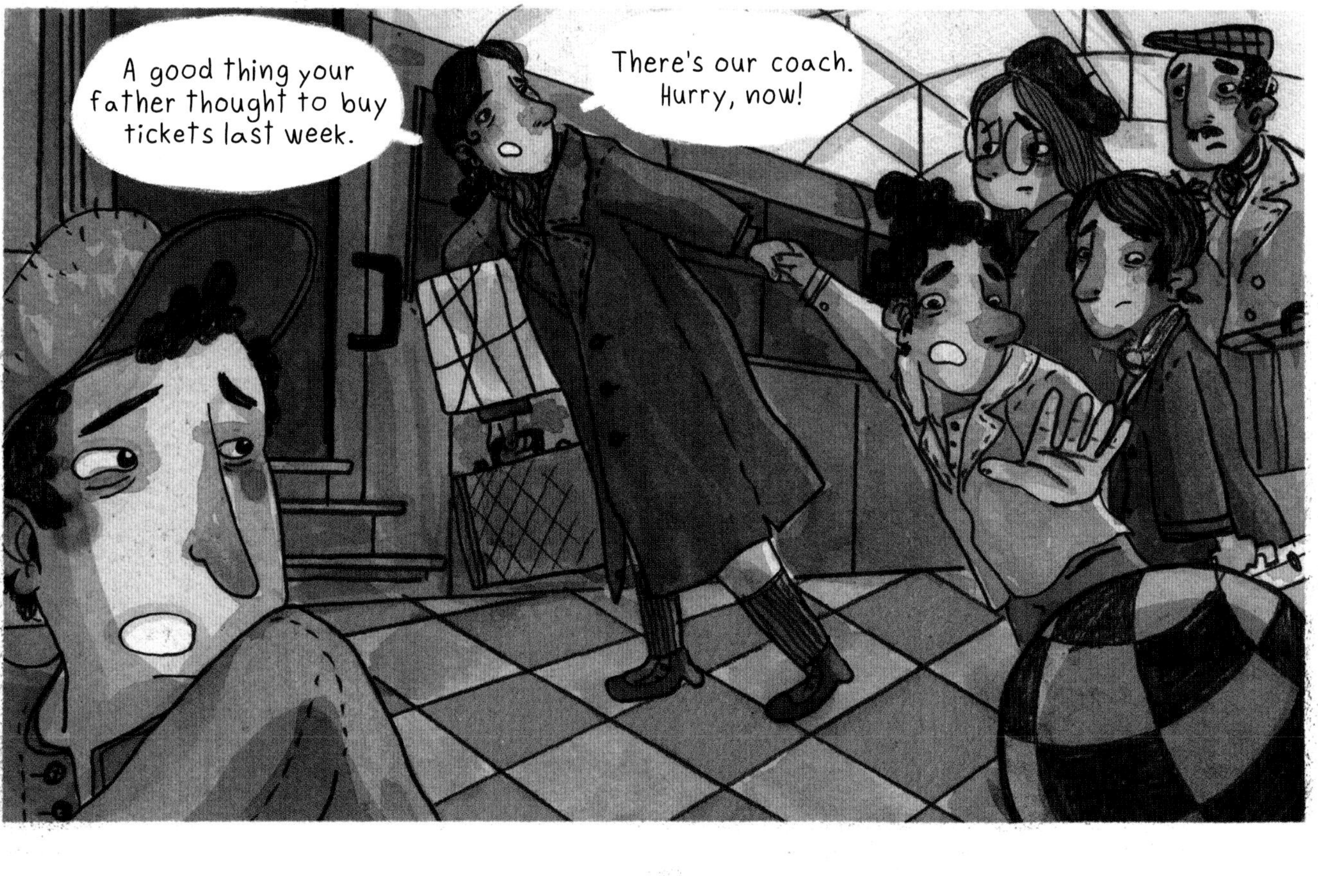
A good thing your father thought to buy tickets last week.
There's our coach. Hurry, now!

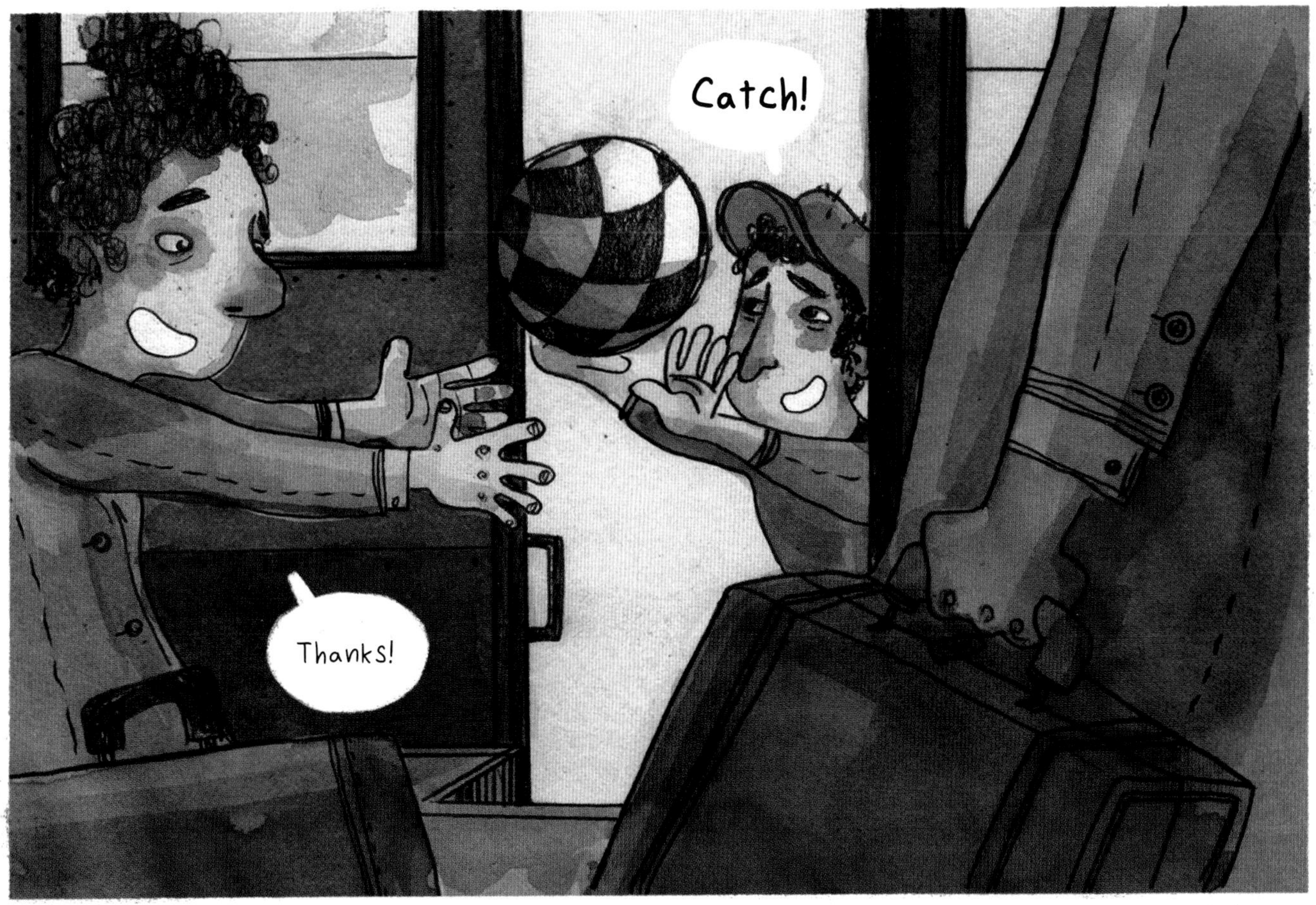
Catch!
Thanks!

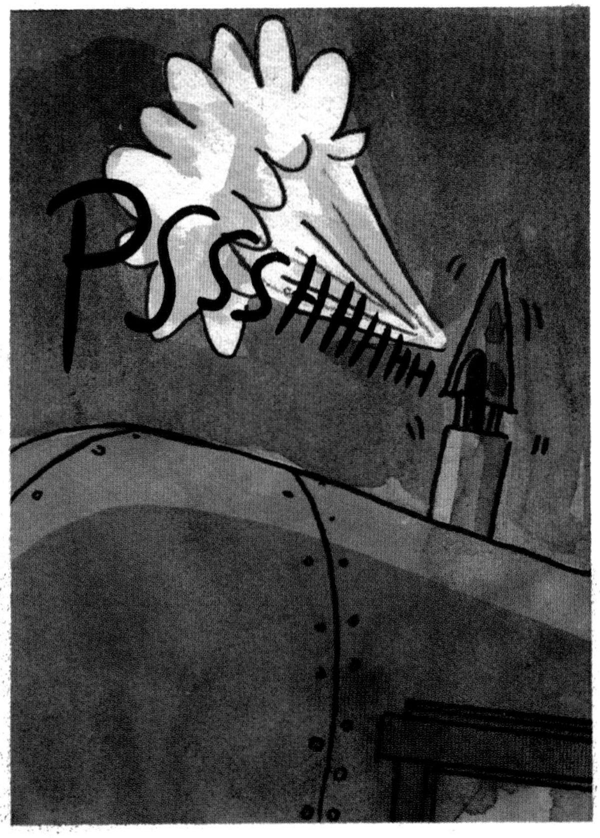
PSSSHHHHHH

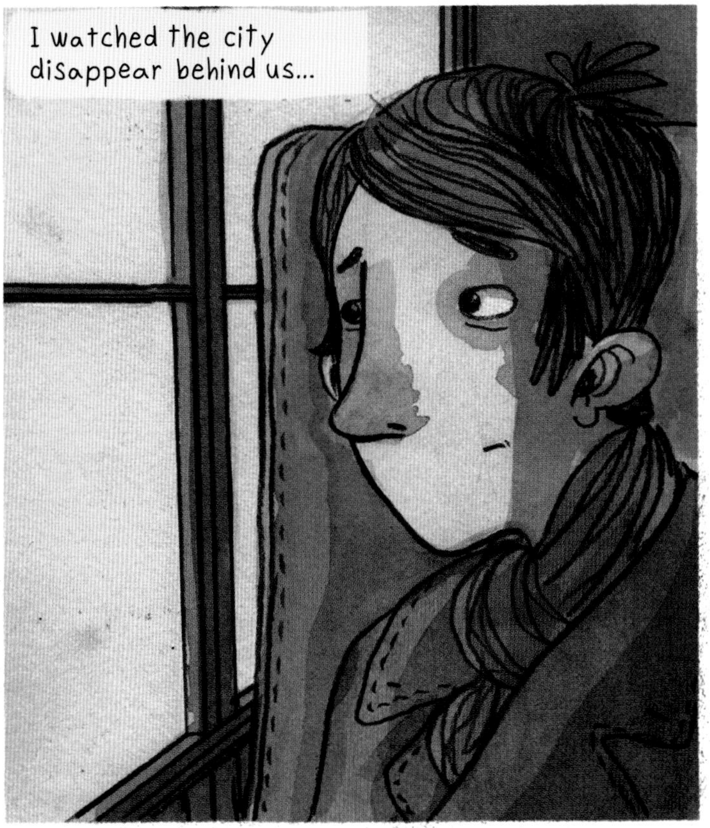
I watched the city disappear behind us...

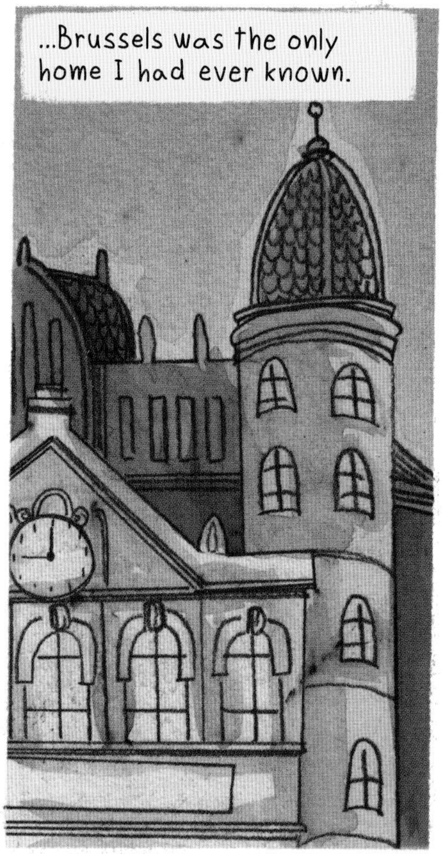
...Brussels was the only home I had ever known.

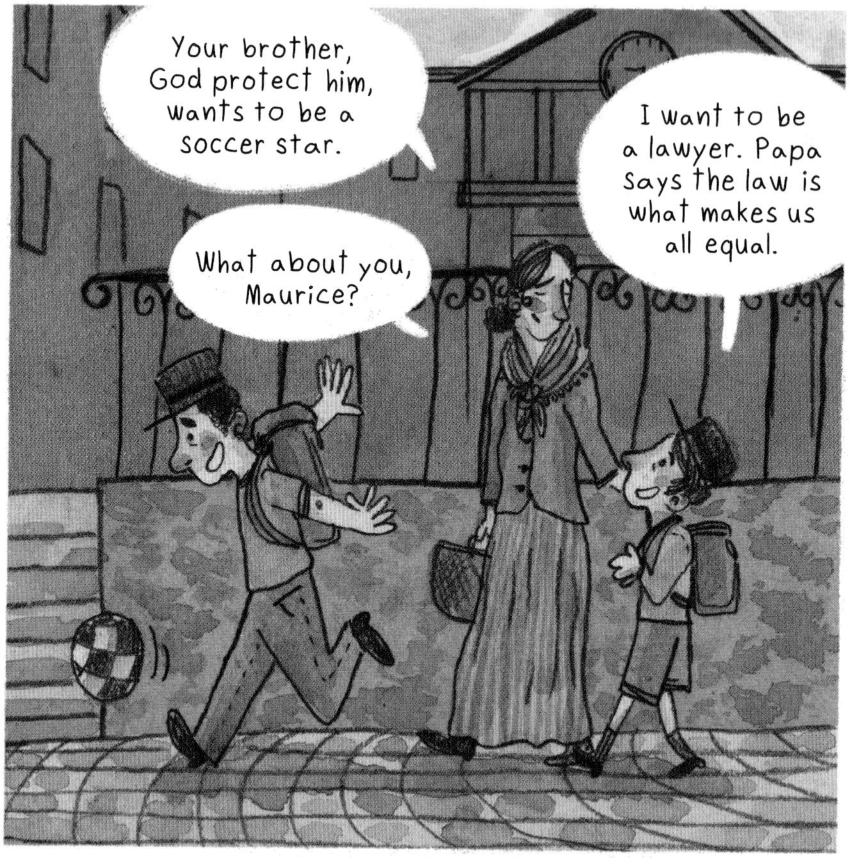
Your brother, God protect him, wants to be a soccer star.
What about you, Maurice?
I want to be a lawyer. Papa says the law is what makes us all equal.

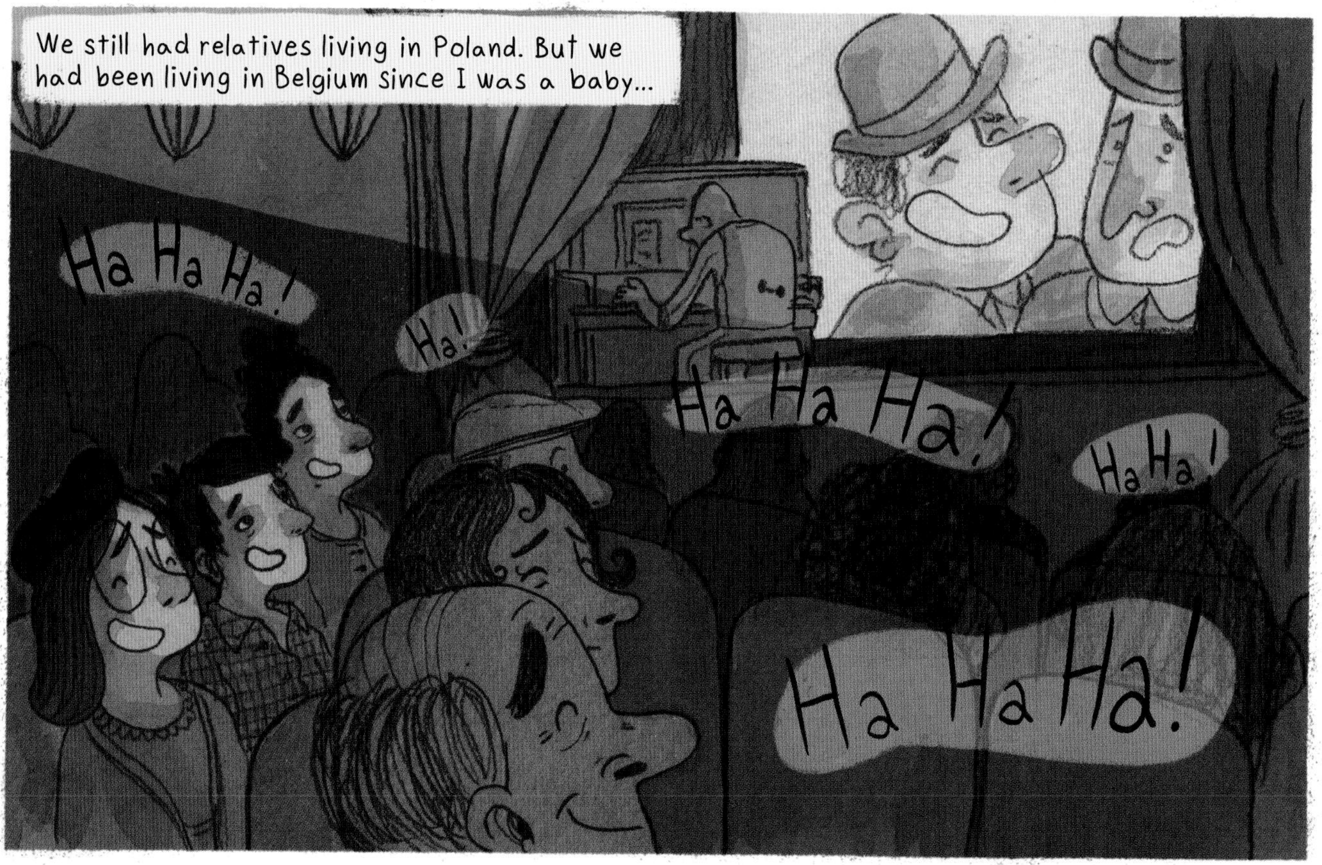
We still had relatives living in Poland. But we had been living in Belgium since I was a baby...
Ha Ha Ha!
Ha!
Ha Ha Ha!
Ha Ha!
Ha Ha Ha!

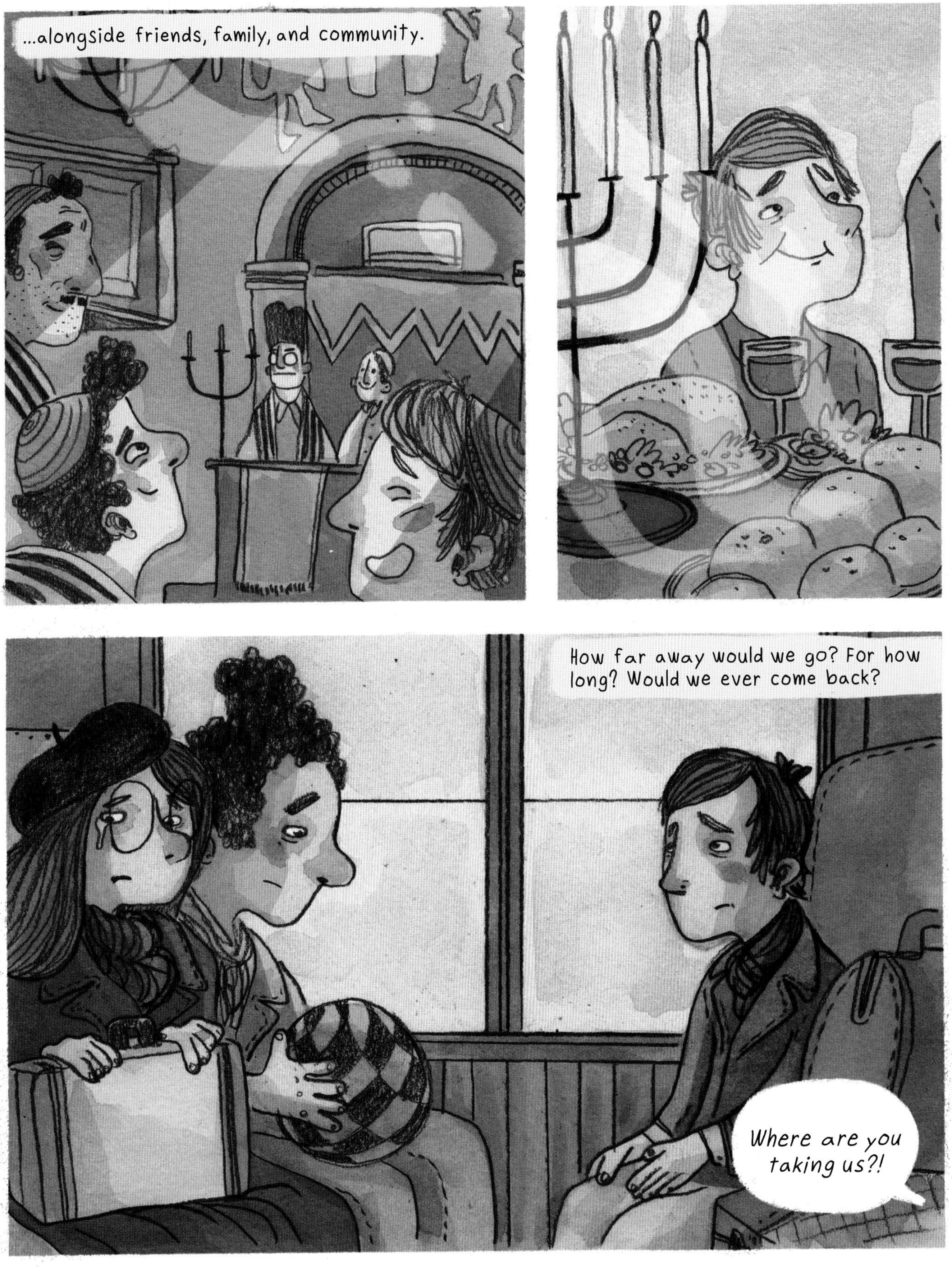
...alongside friends, family, and community.
How far away would we go? For how long? Would we ever come back?
Where are you taking us?!

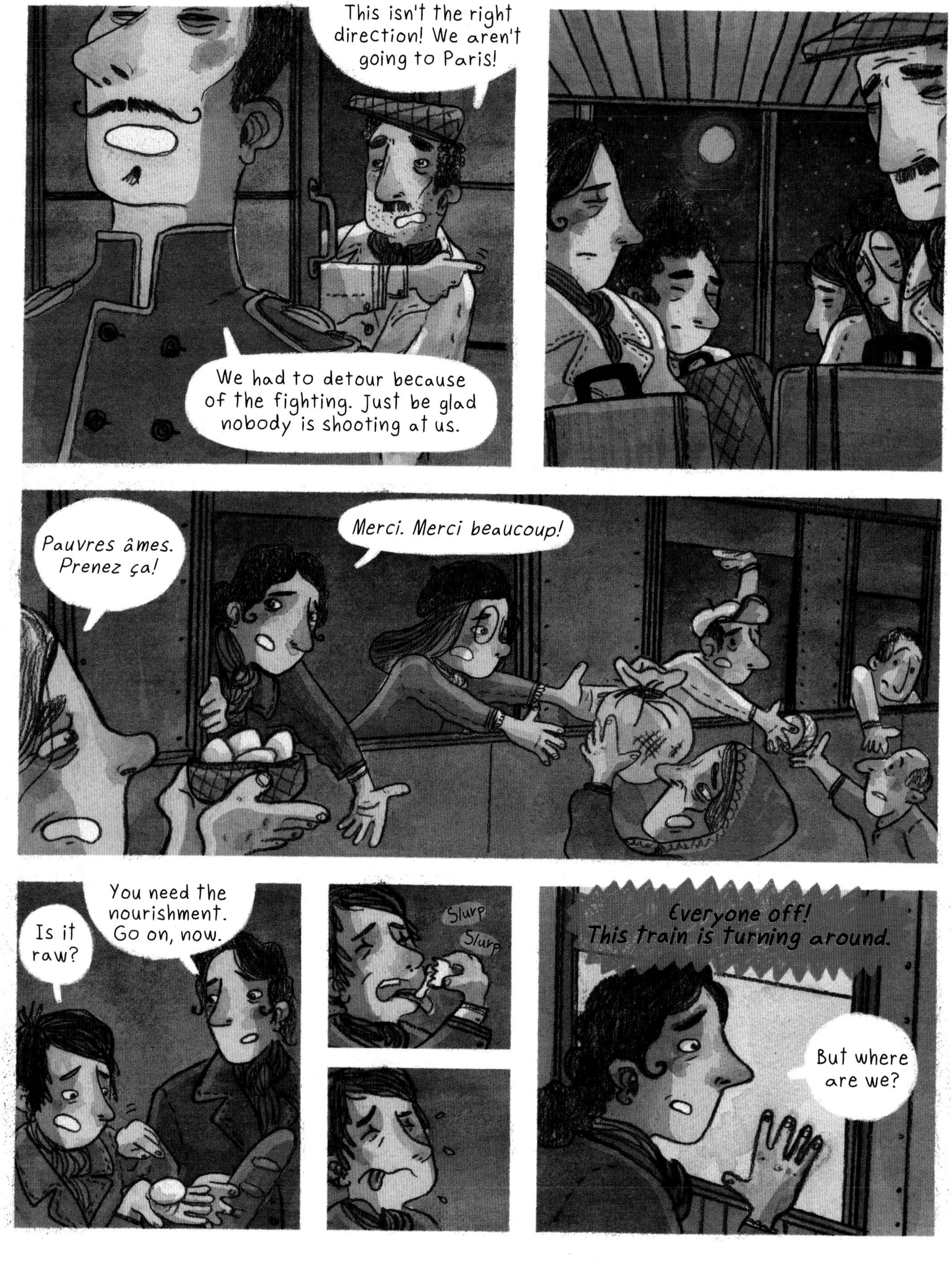
This isn't the right direction! We aren't going to Paris!
We had to detour because of the fighting. Just be glad nobody is shooting at us.
Pauvres âmes. Prenez ça!
Merci. Merci beaucoup!
You need the nourishment. Go on, now.
Is it raw?
Slurp
Slurp
Everyone off! This train is turning around.
But where are we?

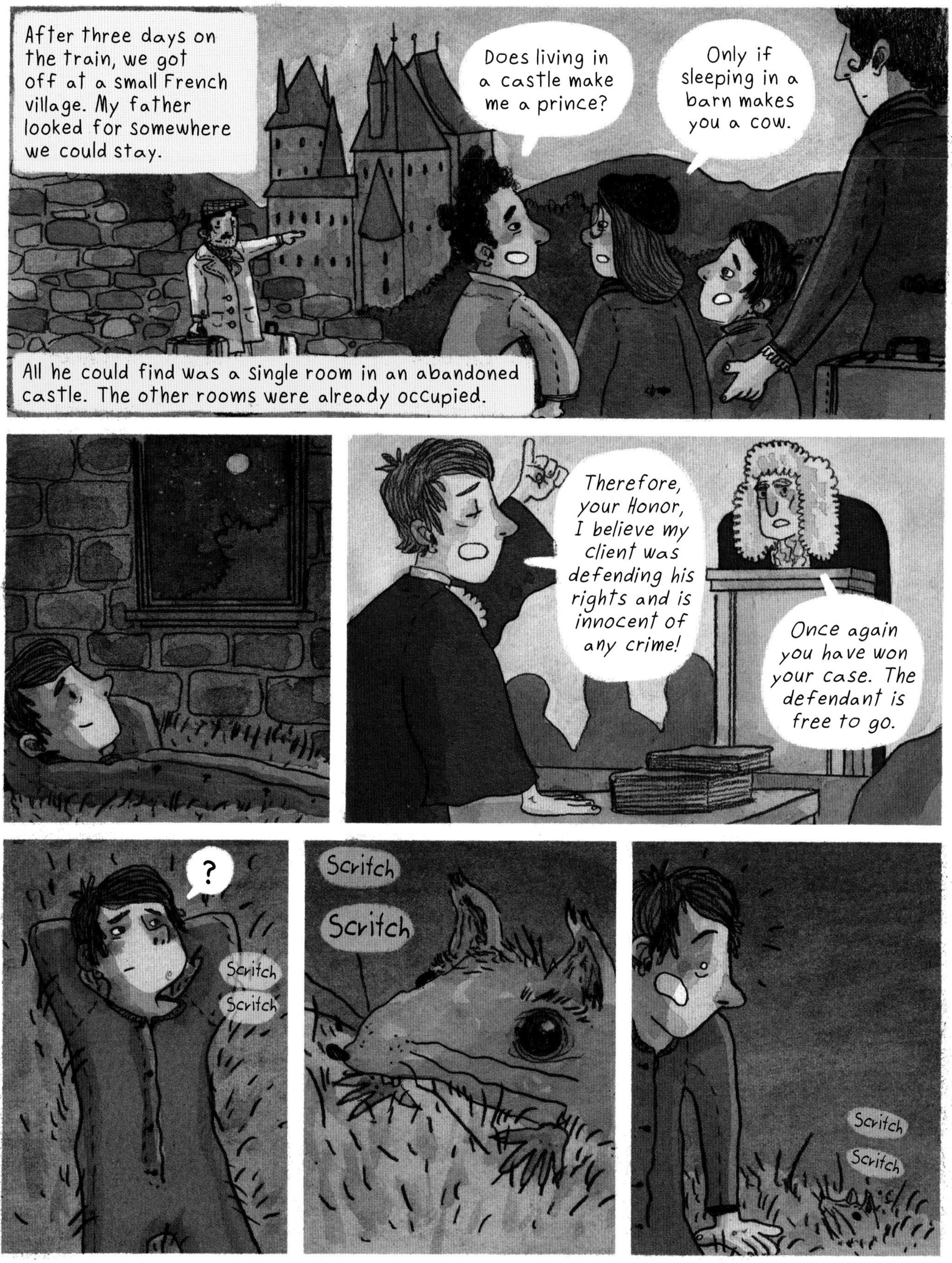
After three days on the train, we got off at a small French village. My father looked for somewhere we could stay.
Does living in a castle make me a prince?
Only if sleeping in a barn makes you a cow.
All he could find was a single room in an abandoned castle. The other rooms were already occupied.
Therefore, your Honor, I believe my client was defending his rights and is innocent of any crime!
Once again you have won your case. The defendant is free to go.
?
Scritch
Scritch
Scritch
Scritch
Scritch
Scritch

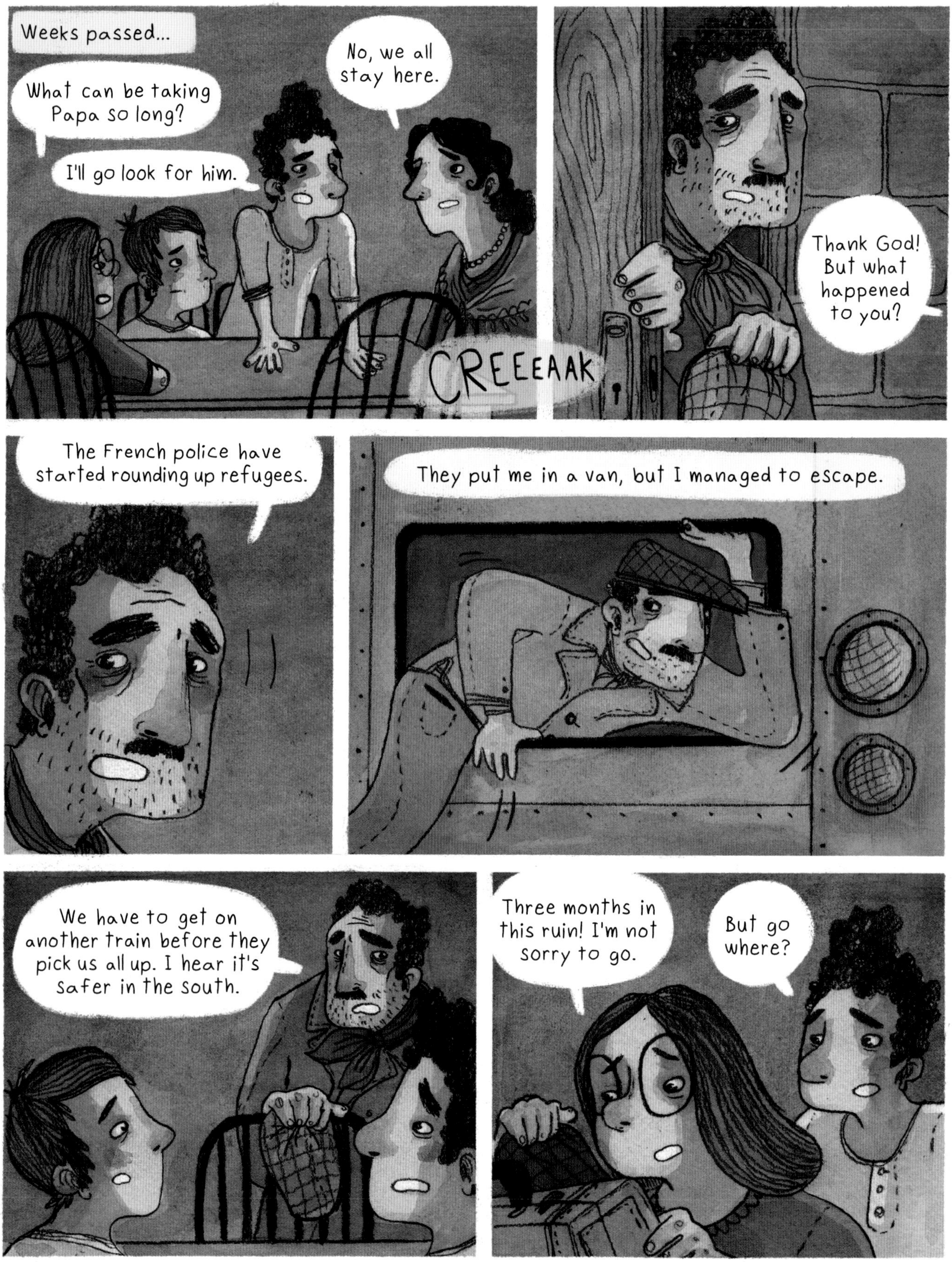

Weeks passed...
What can be taking Papa so long?
No, we all stay here.
I'll go look for him.
CREEEAAK
Thank God! But what happened to you?
The French police have started rounding up refugees.
They put me in a van, but I managed to escape.
We have to get on another train before they pick us all up. I hear it's safer in the south.
Three months in this ruin! I'm not sorry to go.
But go where?

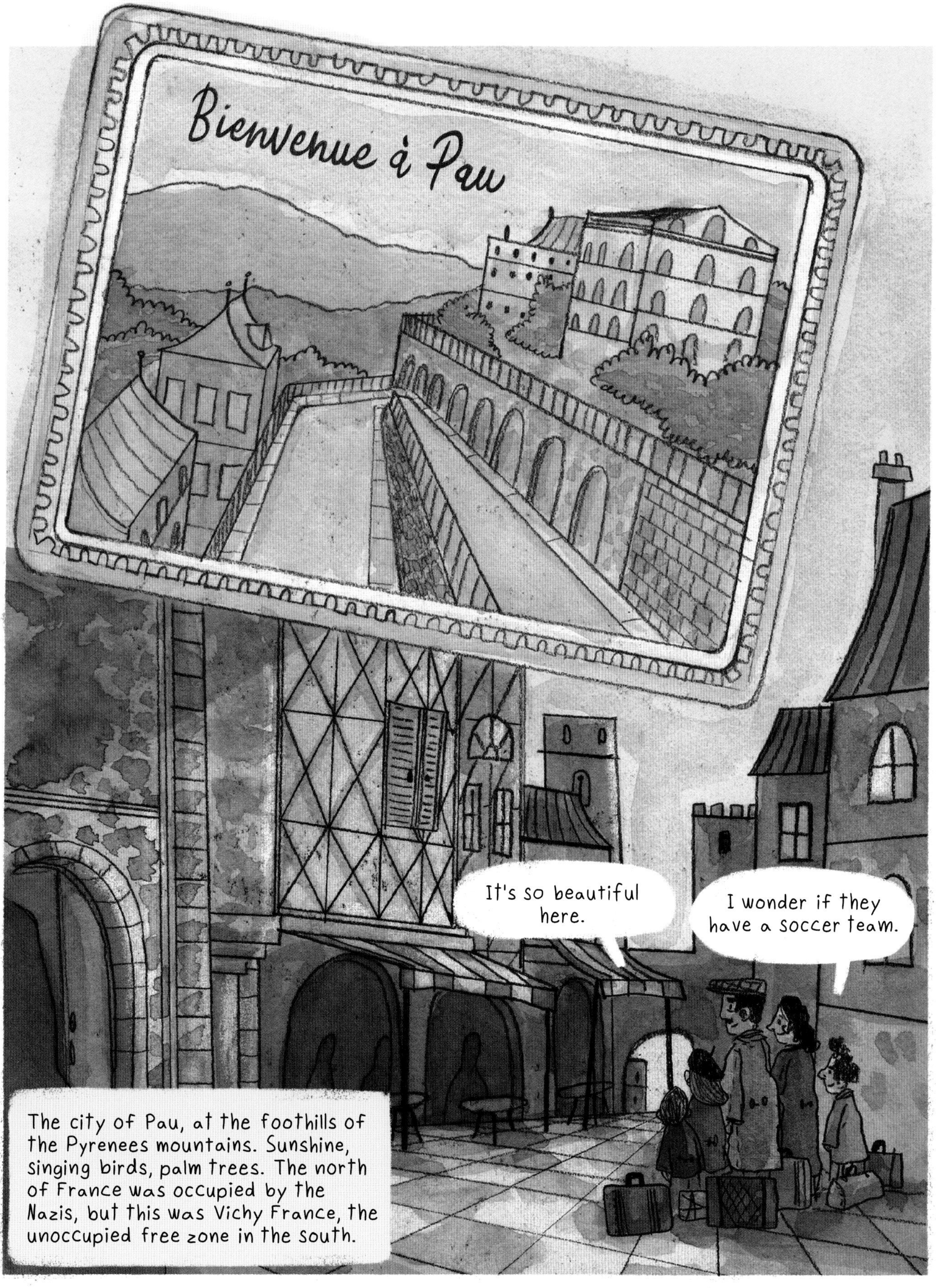
Bienvenue à Pau
It's so beautiful here.
I wonder if they have a soccer team.
The city of Pau, at the foothills of the Pyrenees mountains. Sunshine, singing birds, palm trees. The north of France was occupied by the Nazis, but this was Vichy France, the unoccupied free zone in the south.

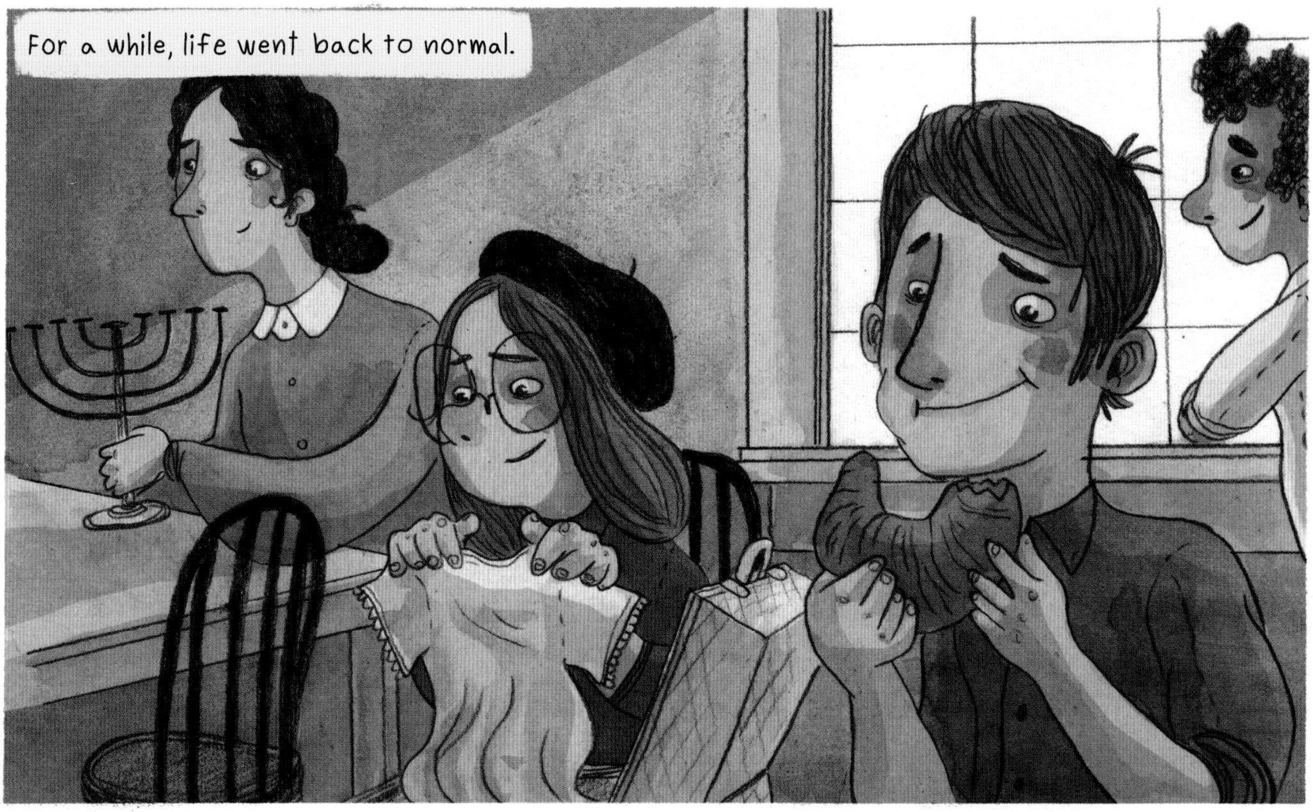
For a while, life went back to normal.

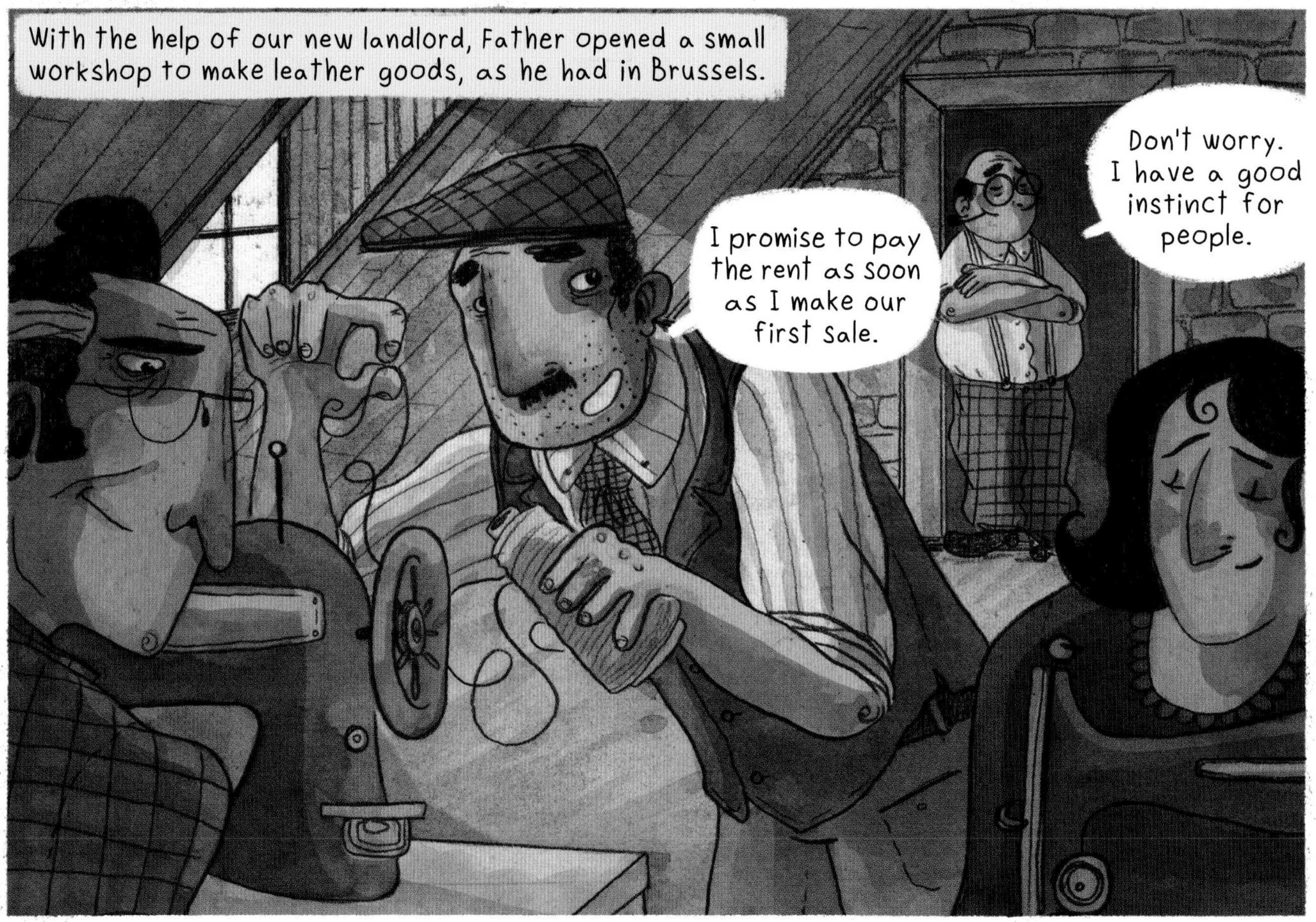
With the help of our new landlord, Father opened a small workshop to make leather goods, as he had in Brussels.
I promise to pay the rent as soon as I make our first sale.
Don't worry. I have a good instinct for people.

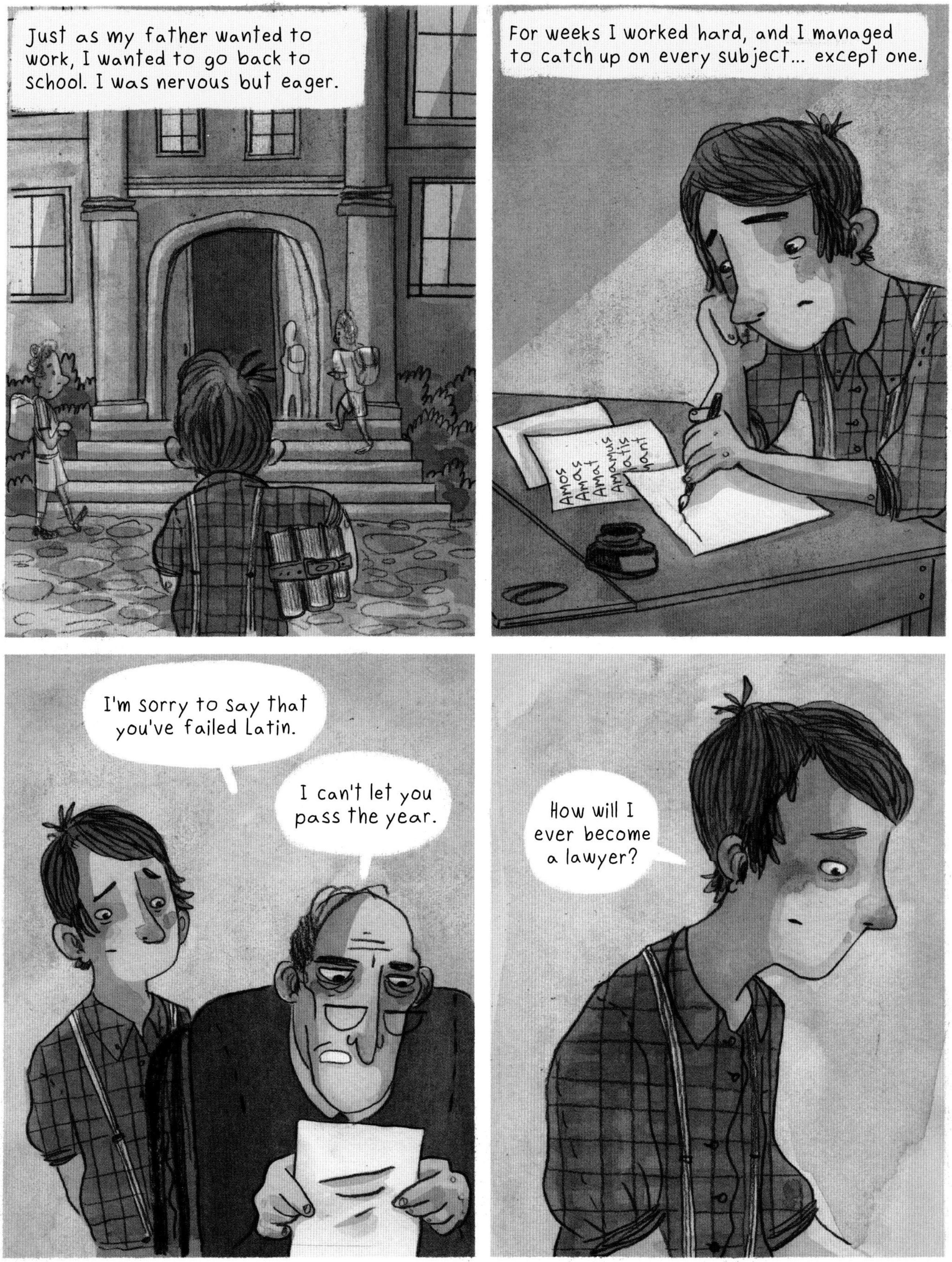
Just as my father wanted to work, I wanted to go back to school. I was nervous but eager.
For weeks I worked hard, and I managed to catch up on every subject... except one.
Amos
Amas
Amat
Amamus
I'm sorry to say that you've failed Latin.
I can't let you pass the year.
How will I ever become a lawyer?

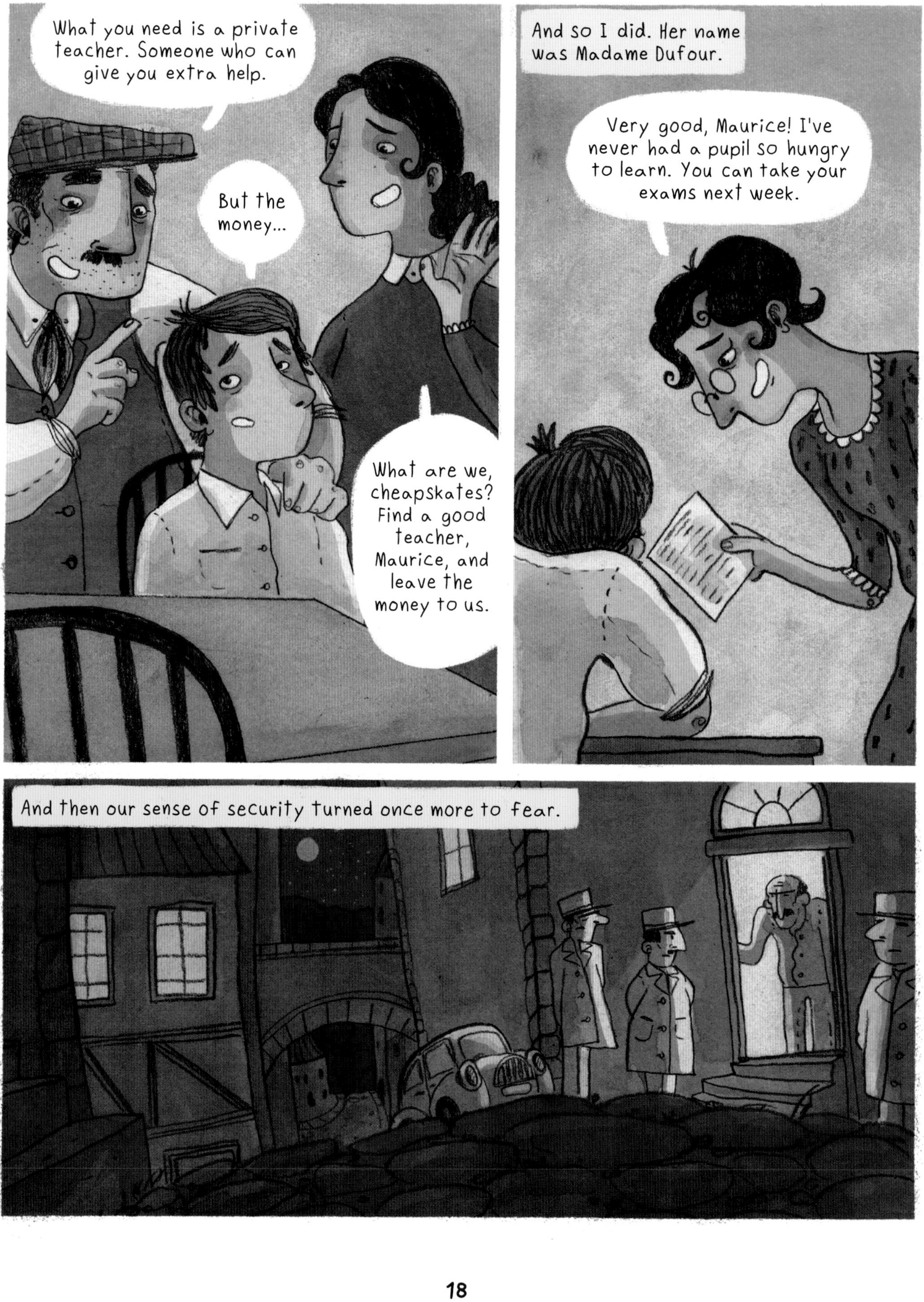
What you need is a private teacher. Someone who can give you extra help.
But the money...
What are we, cheapskates? Find a good teacher, Maurice, and leave the money to us.
And so I did. Her name was Madame Dufour.
Very good, Maurice! I've never had a pupil so hungry to learn. You can take your exams next week.
And then our sense of security turned once more to fear.

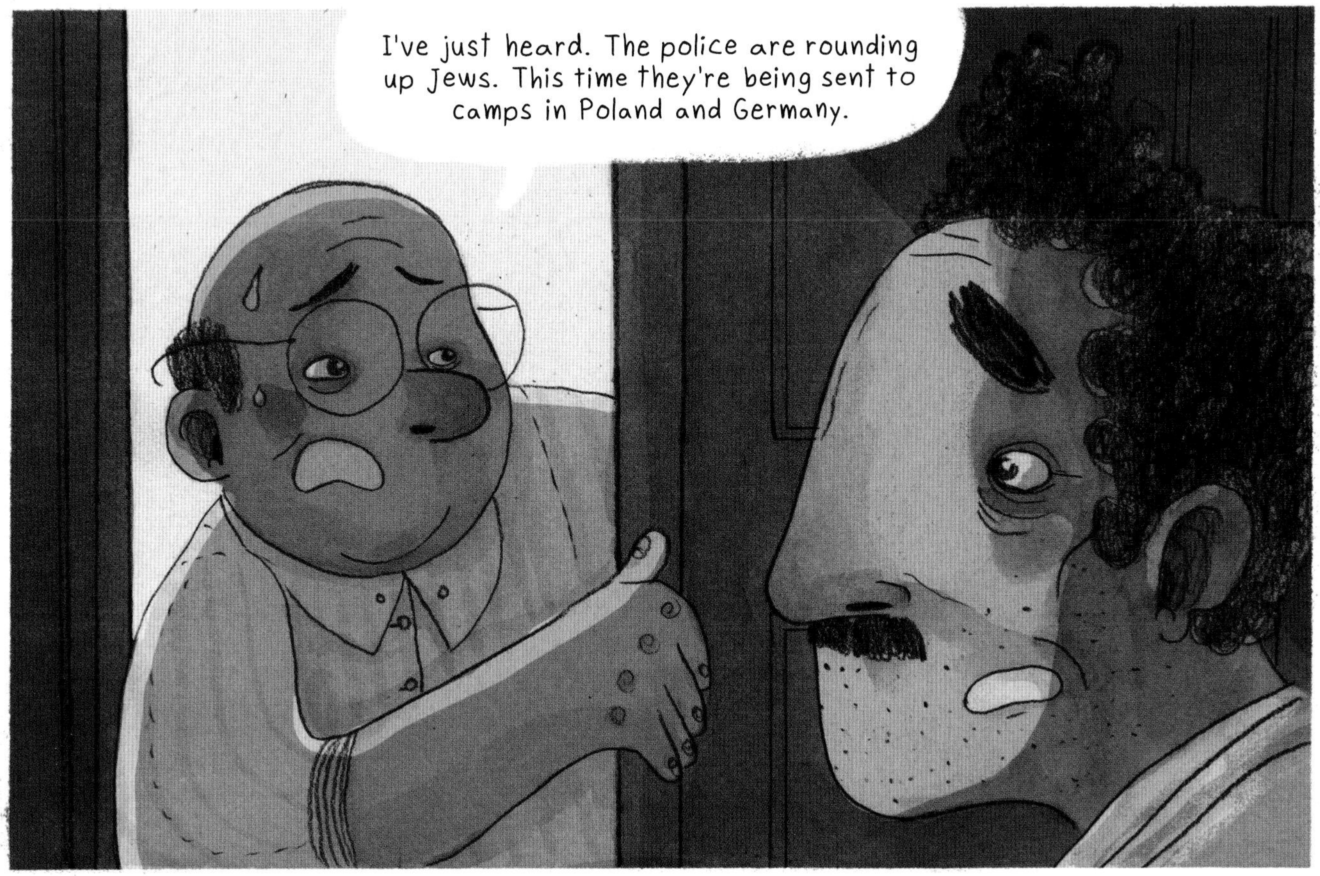
I've just heard. The police are rounding up Jews. This time they're being sent to camps in Poland and Germany.

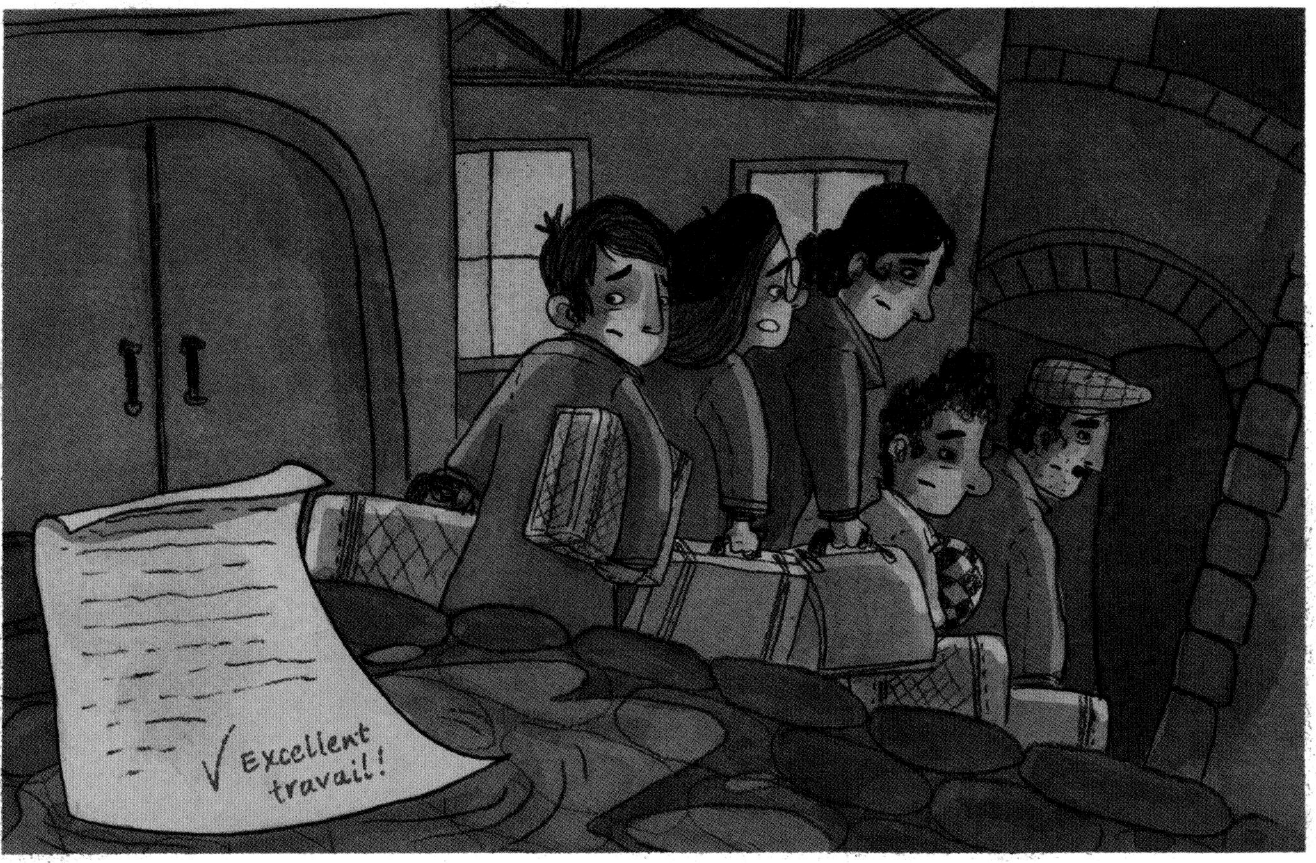
Excellent travail!

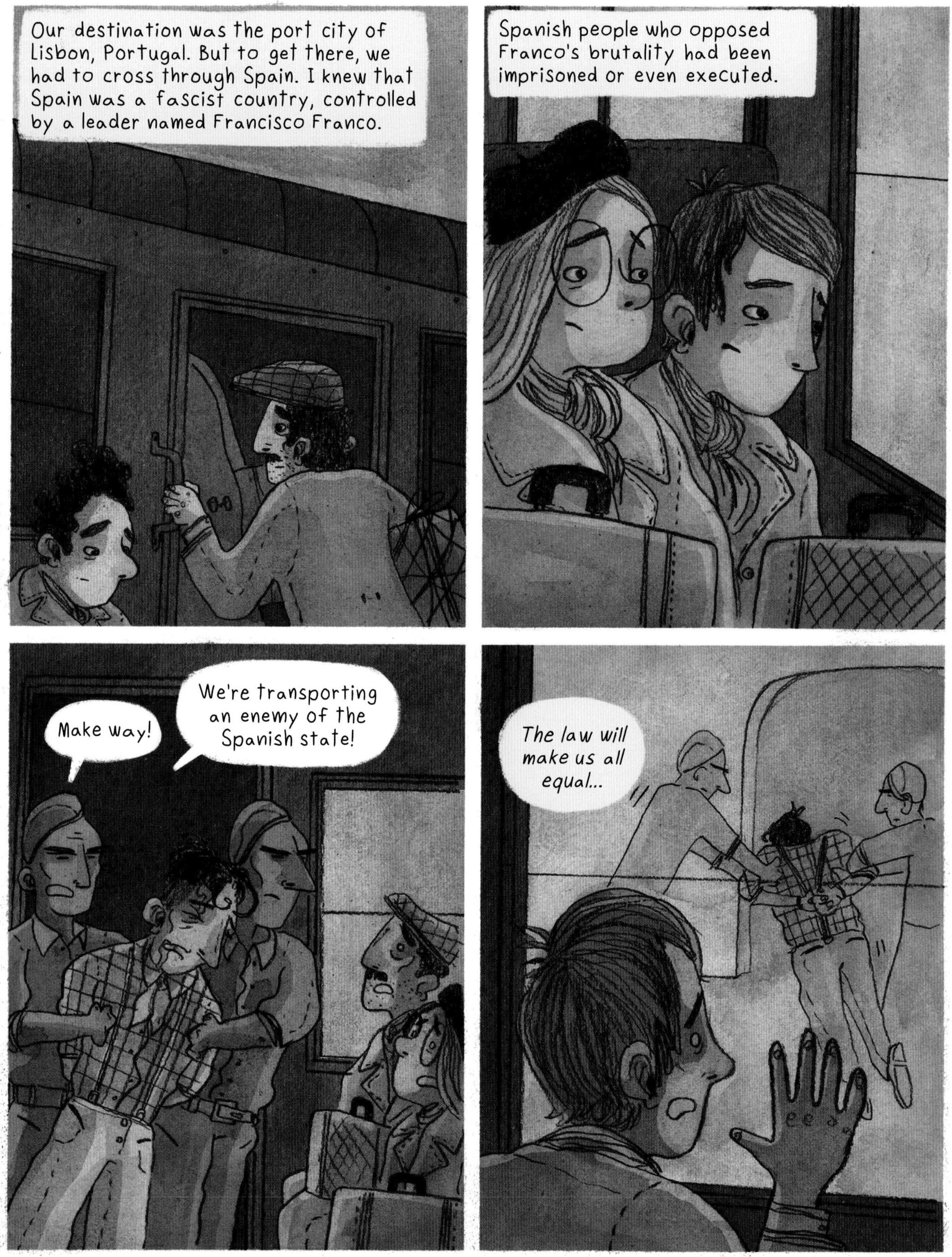
Our destination was the port city of Lisbon, Portugal. But to get there, we had to cross through Spain. I knew that Spain was a fascist country, controlled by a leader named Francisco Franco.
Spanish people who opposed Franco's brutality had been imprisoned or even executed.
Make way!
We're transporting an enemy of the Spanish state!
The law will make us all equal...

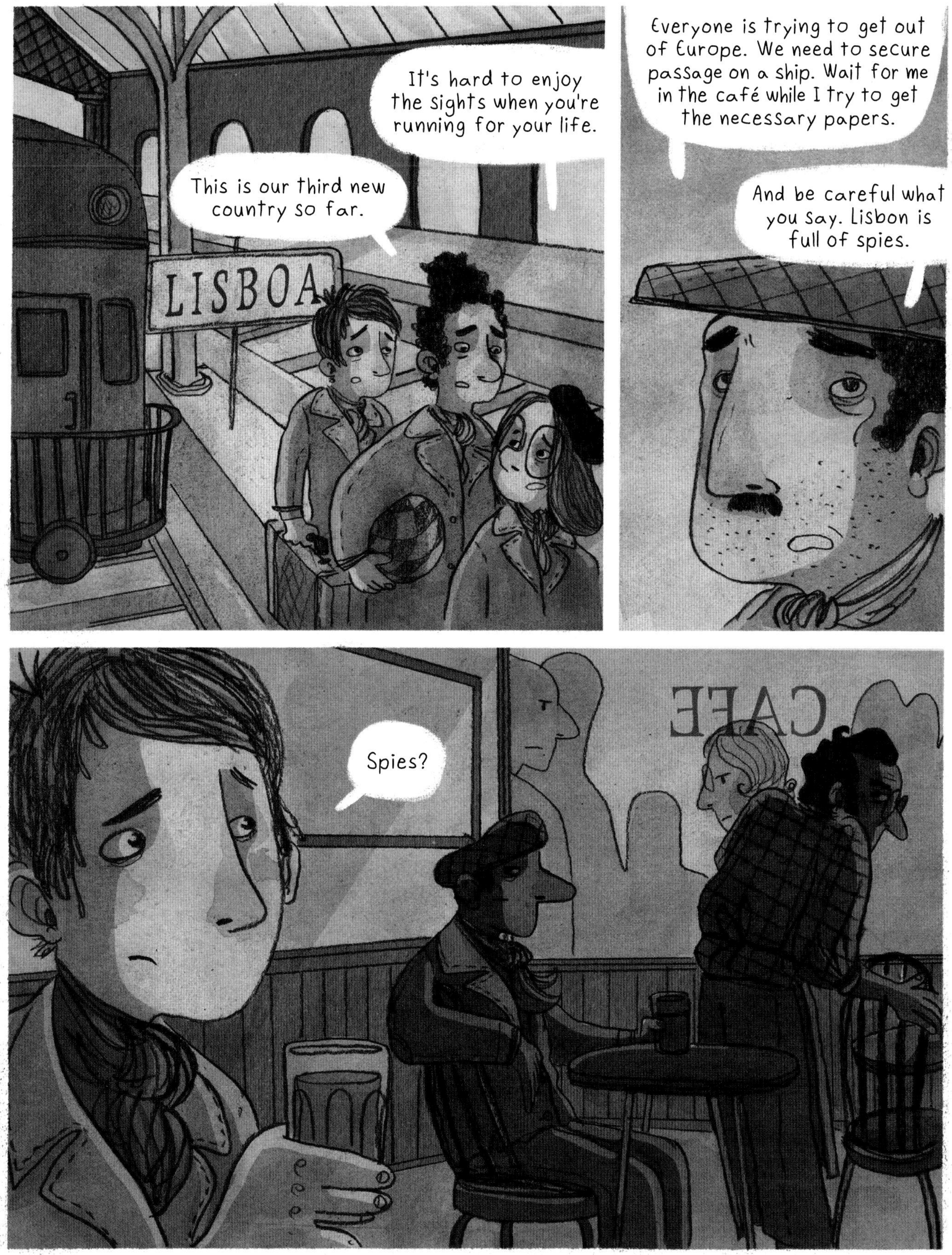

This is our third new country so far.
It's hard to enjoy the sights when you're running for your life.
LISBOA
Everyone is trying to get out of Europe. We need to secure passage on a ship. Wait for me in the café while I try to get the necessary papers.
And be careful what you say. Lisbon is full of spies.
CAFE
Spies?

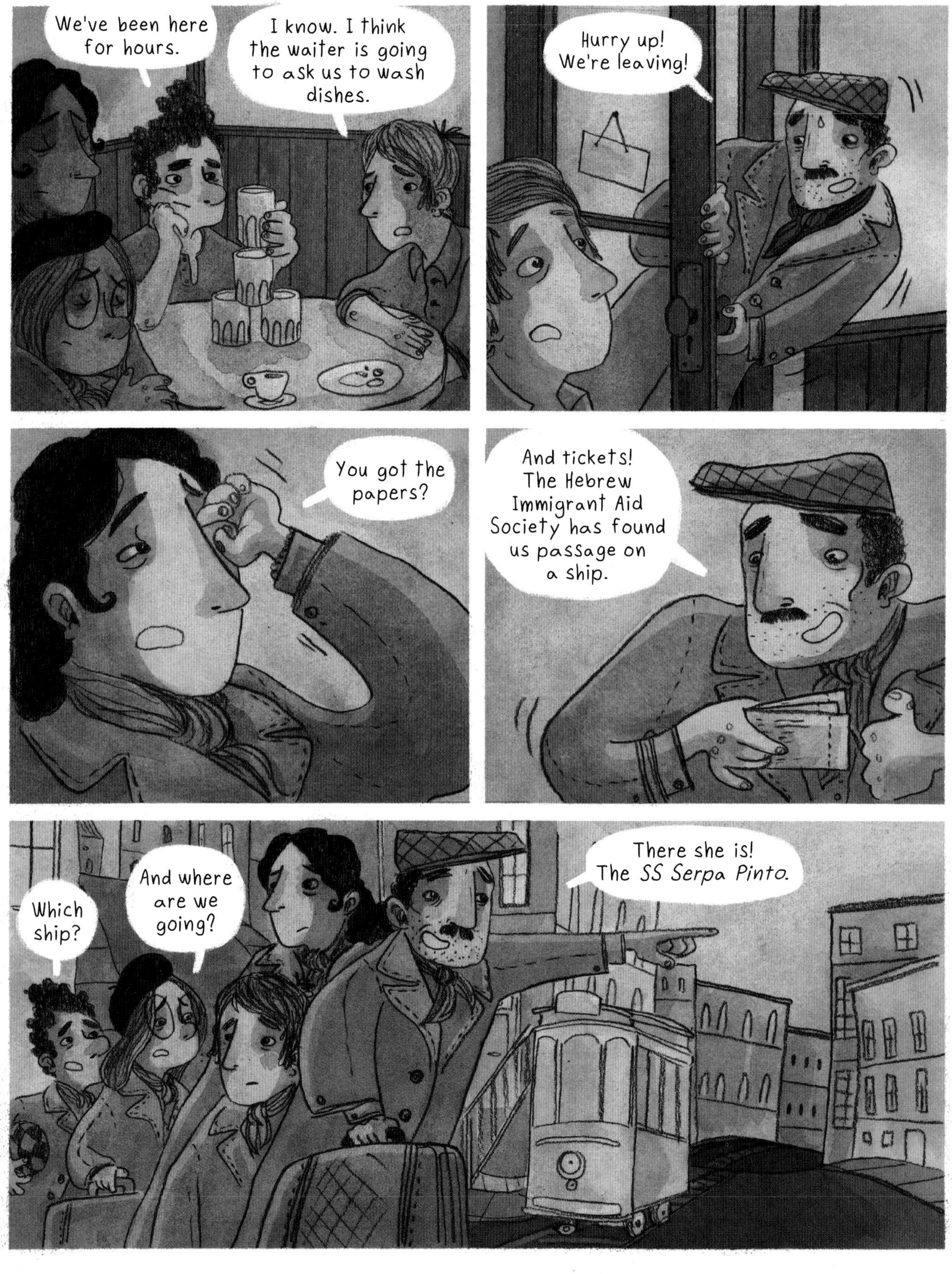
We've been here for hours.
I know. I think the waiter is going to ask us to wash dishes.
Hurry up! We're leaving!
You got the papers?
And tickets! The Hebrew Immigrant Aid Society has found us passage on a ship.
Which ship?
And where are we going?
There she is! The *SS Serpa Pinto*.

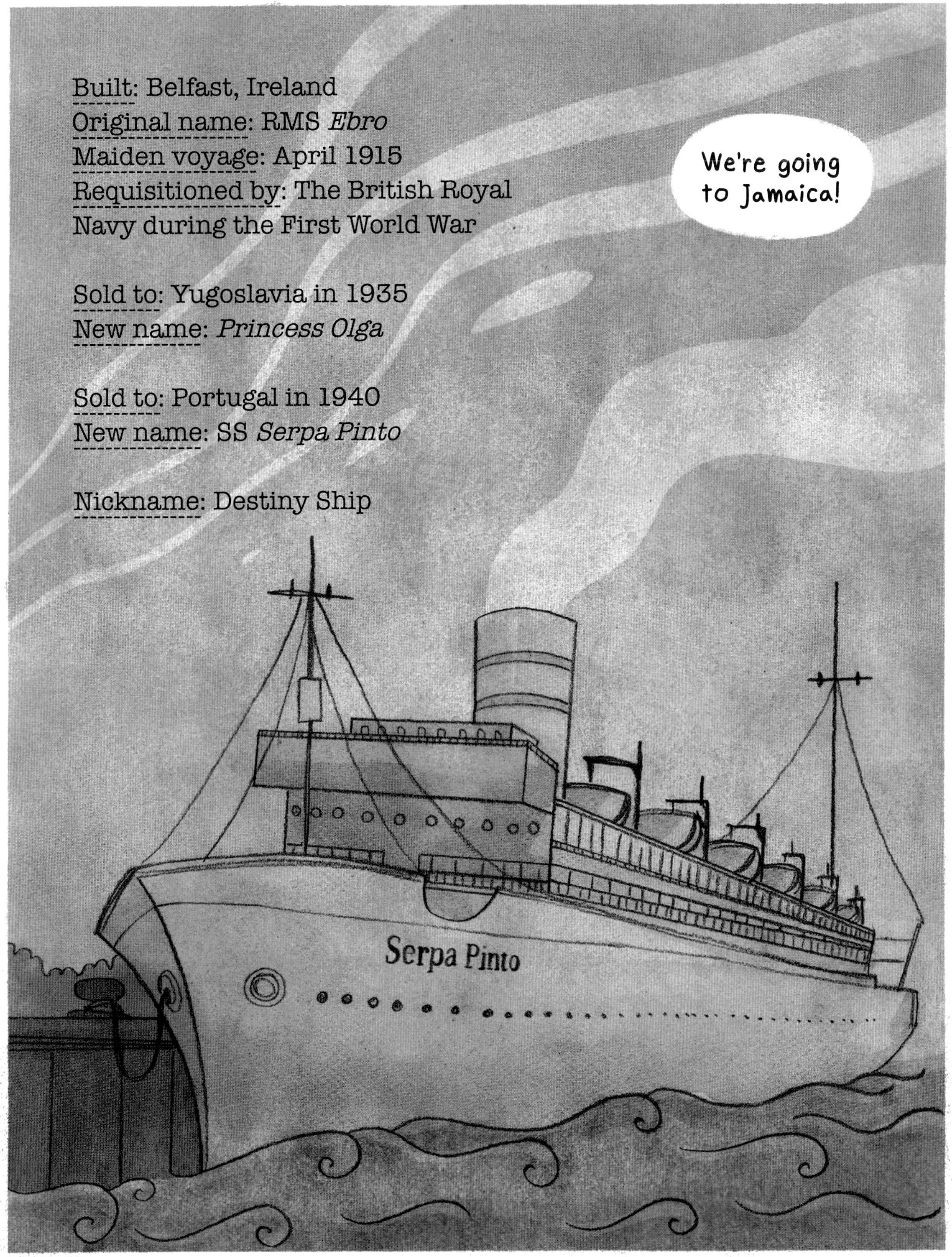
Built: Belfast, Ireland
Original name: RMS *Ebro*
Maiden voyage: April 1915
Requisitioned by: The British Royal Navy during the First World War
Sold to: Yugoslavia in 1935
New name: *Princess Olga*
Sold to: Portugal in 1940
New name: SS *Serpa Pinto*
Nickname: Destiny Ship
We're going to Jamaica!
Serpa Pinto

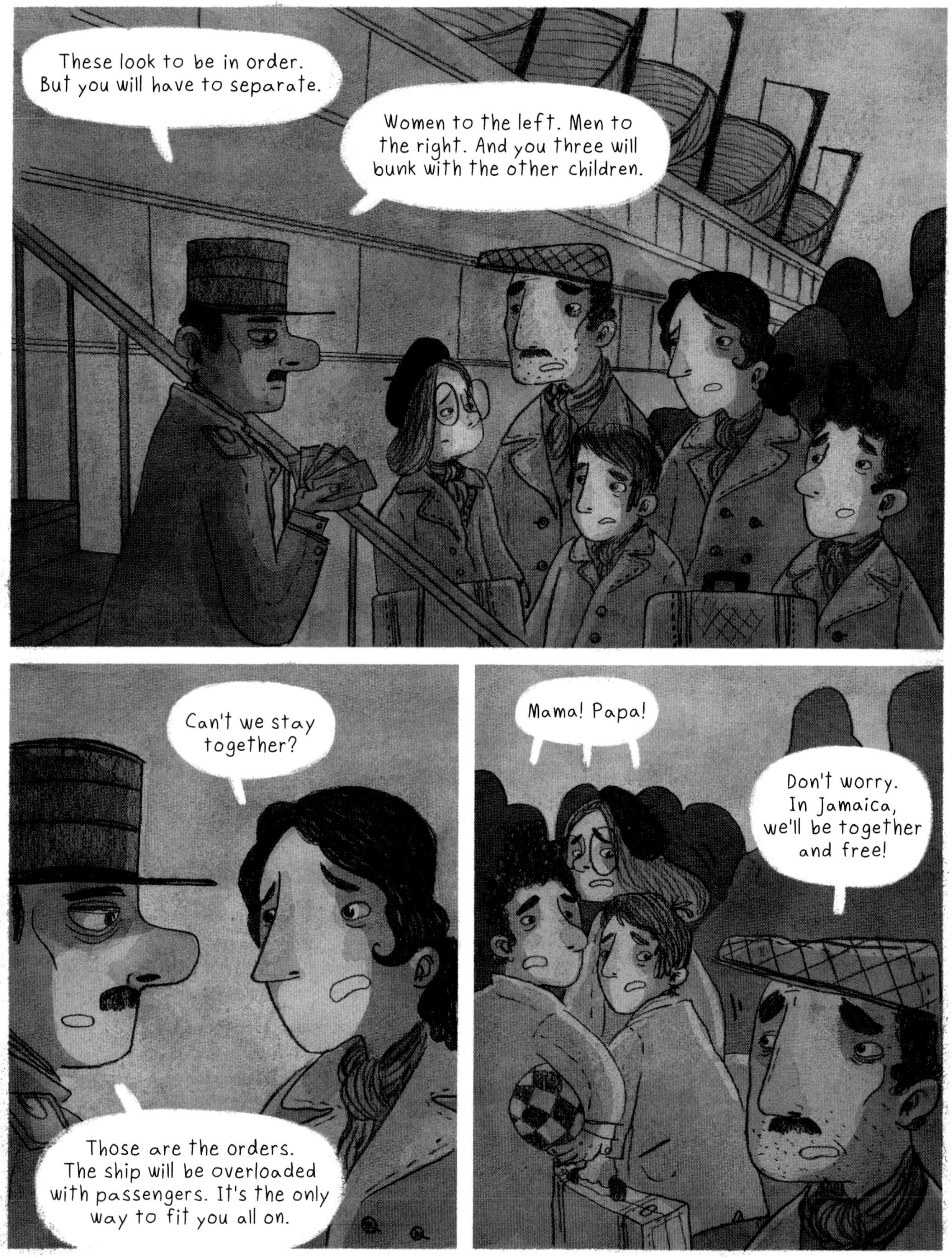
These look to be in order. But you will have to separate.
Women to the left. Men to the right. And you three will bunk with the other children.
Can't we stay together?
Those are the orders. The ship will be overloaded with passengers. It's the only way to fit you all on.
Mama! Papa!
Don't worry. In Jamaica, we'll be together and free!

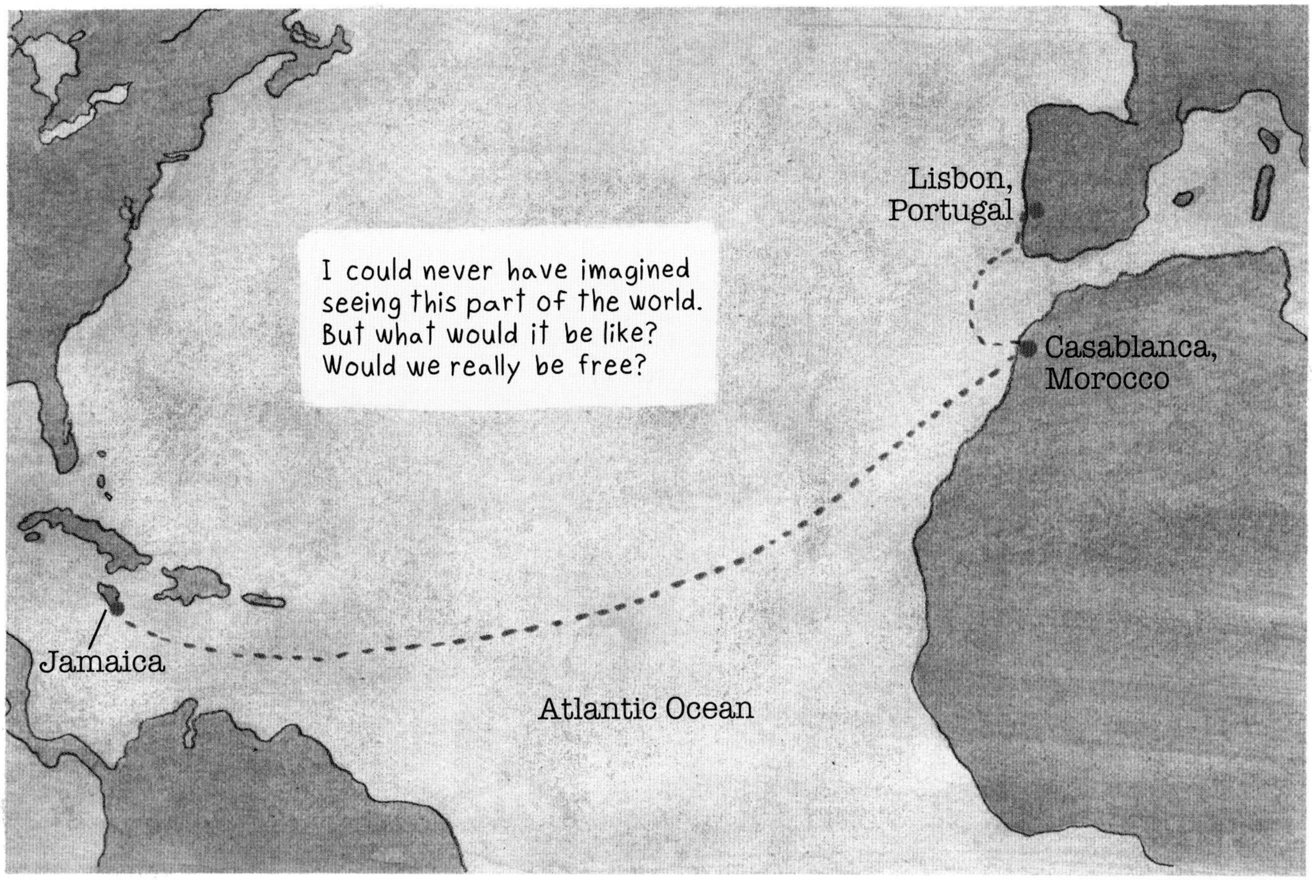
Lisbon, Portugal
I could never have imagined seeing this part of the world. But what would it be like? Would we really be free?
Casablanca, Morocco
Jamaica
Atlantic Ocean

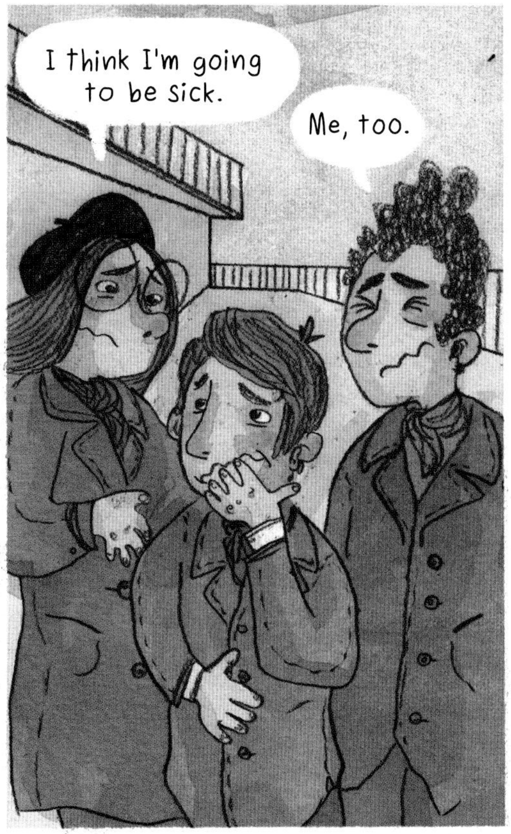
I think I'm going to be sick.
Me, too.

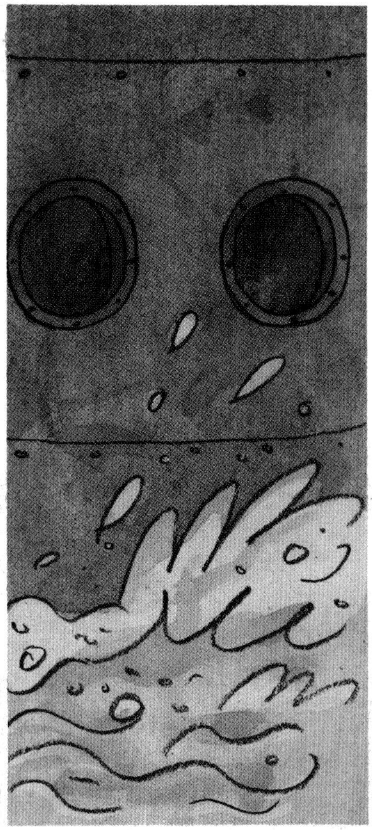

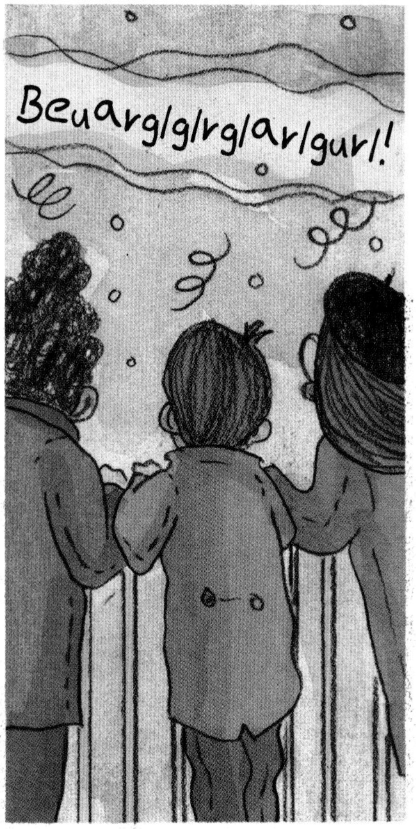
Beuarglglrglarlgurl!

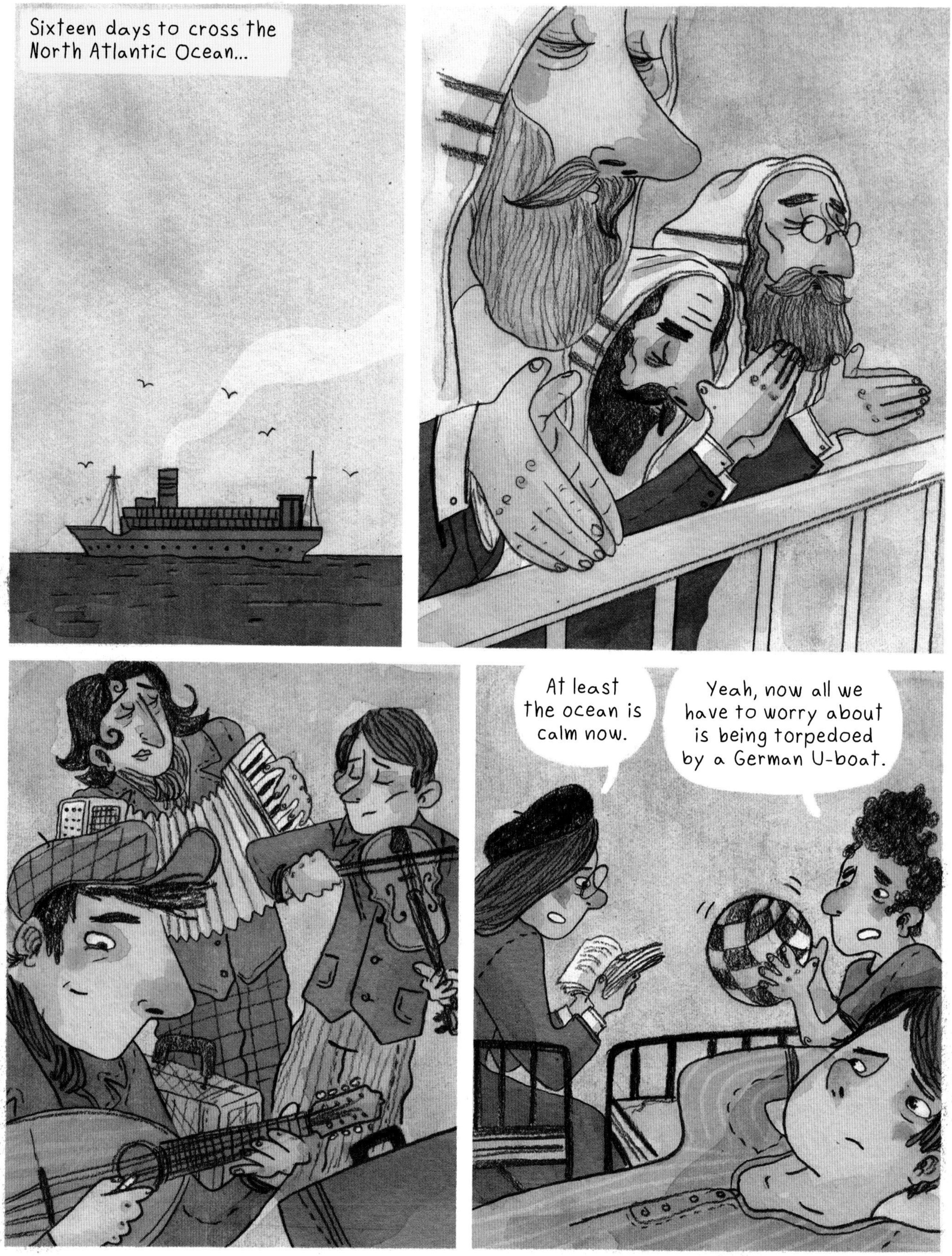
Sixteen days to cross the North Atlantic Ocean...
At least the ocean is calm now.
Yeah, now all we have to worry about is being torpedoed by a German U-boat.

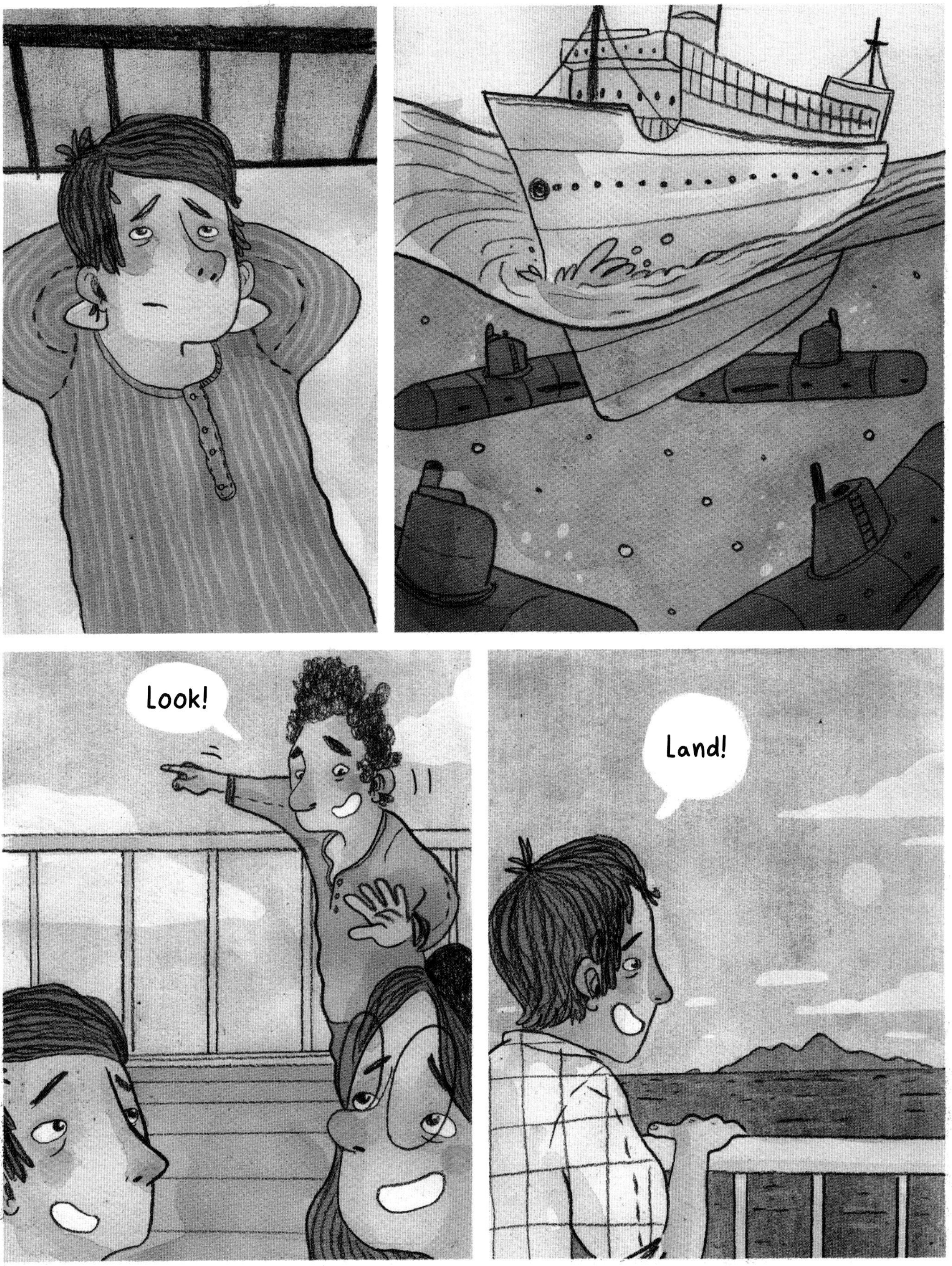
Look!
Land!

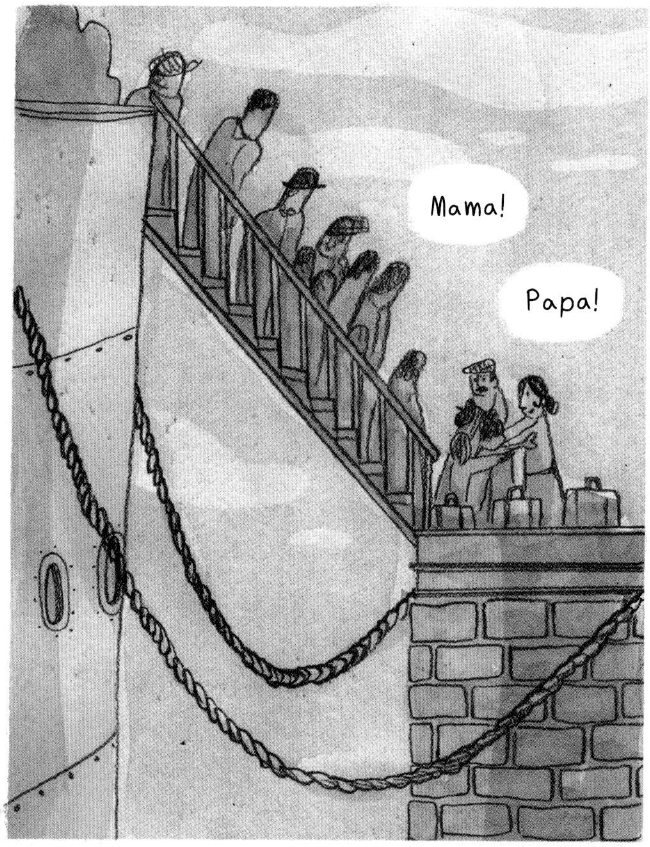
Mama!
Papa!

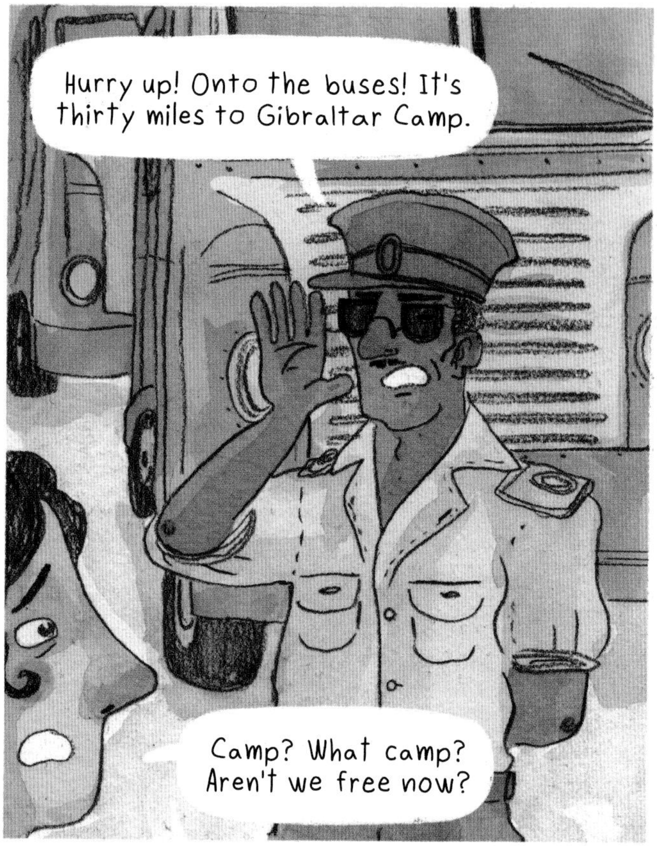
Hurry up! Onto the buses! It's thirty miles to Gibraltar Camp.
Camp? What camp? Aren't we free now?

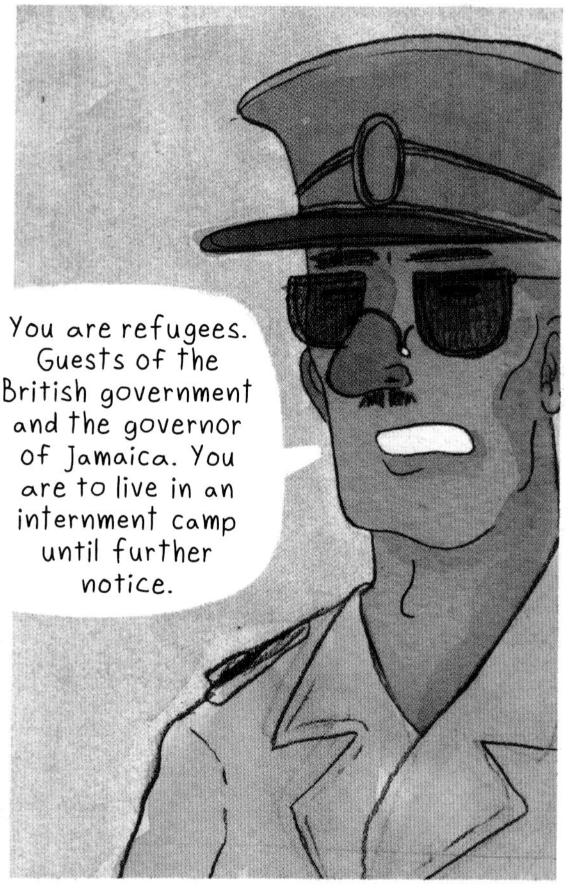
You are refugees. Guests of the British government and the governor of Jamaica. You are to live in an internment camp until further notice.

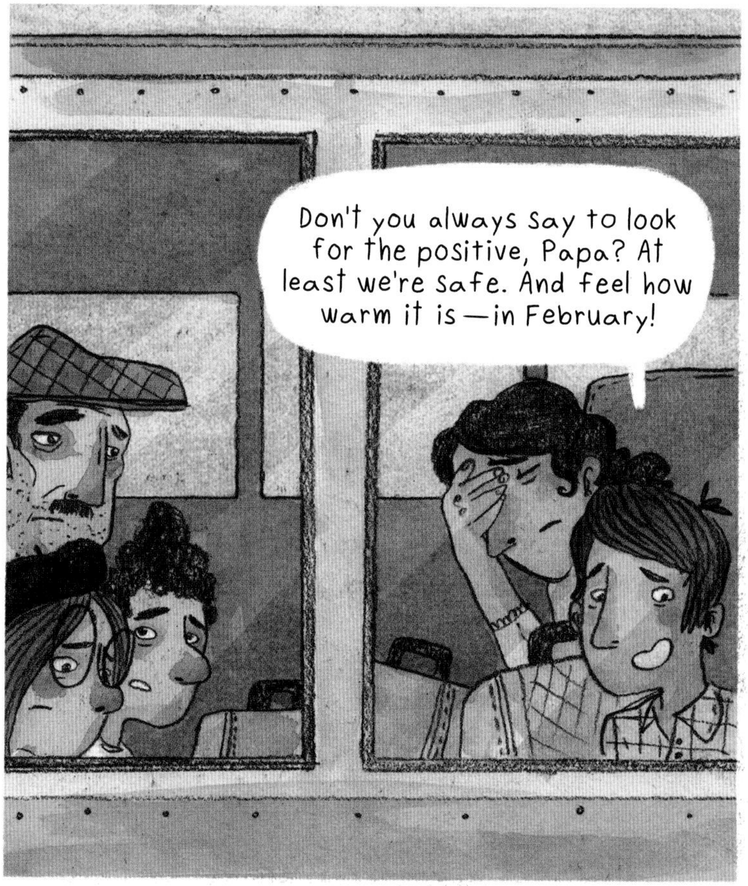
Don't you always say to look for the positive, Papa? At least we're safe. And feel how warm it is—in February!

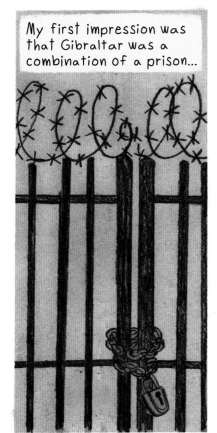

My first impression was that Gibraltar was a combination of a prison...

...and a holiday camp.

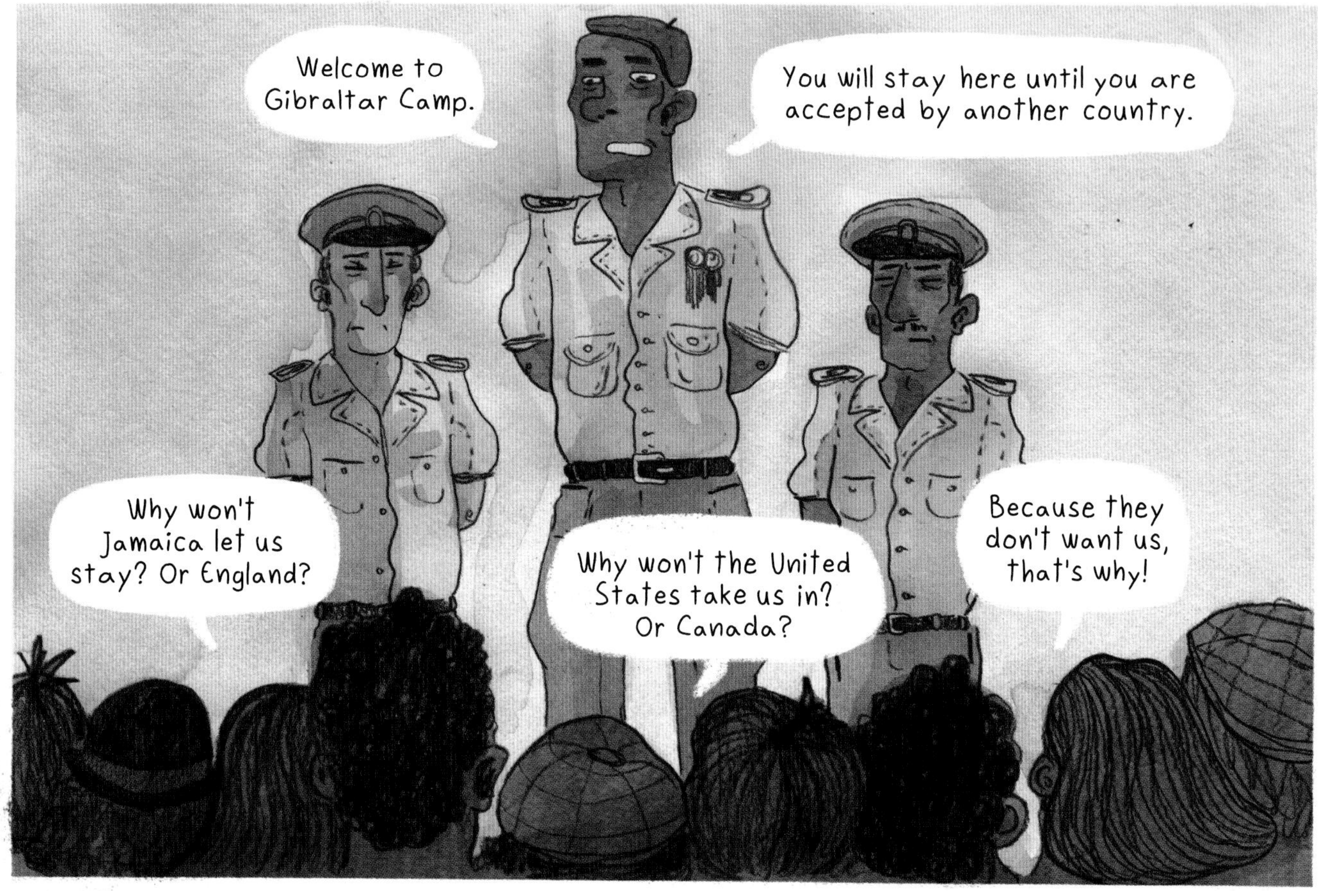
Welcome to Gibraltar Camp.
You will stay here until you are accepted by another country.
Why won't Jamaica let us stay? Or England?
Why won't the United States take us in? Or Canada?
Because they don't want us, that's why!

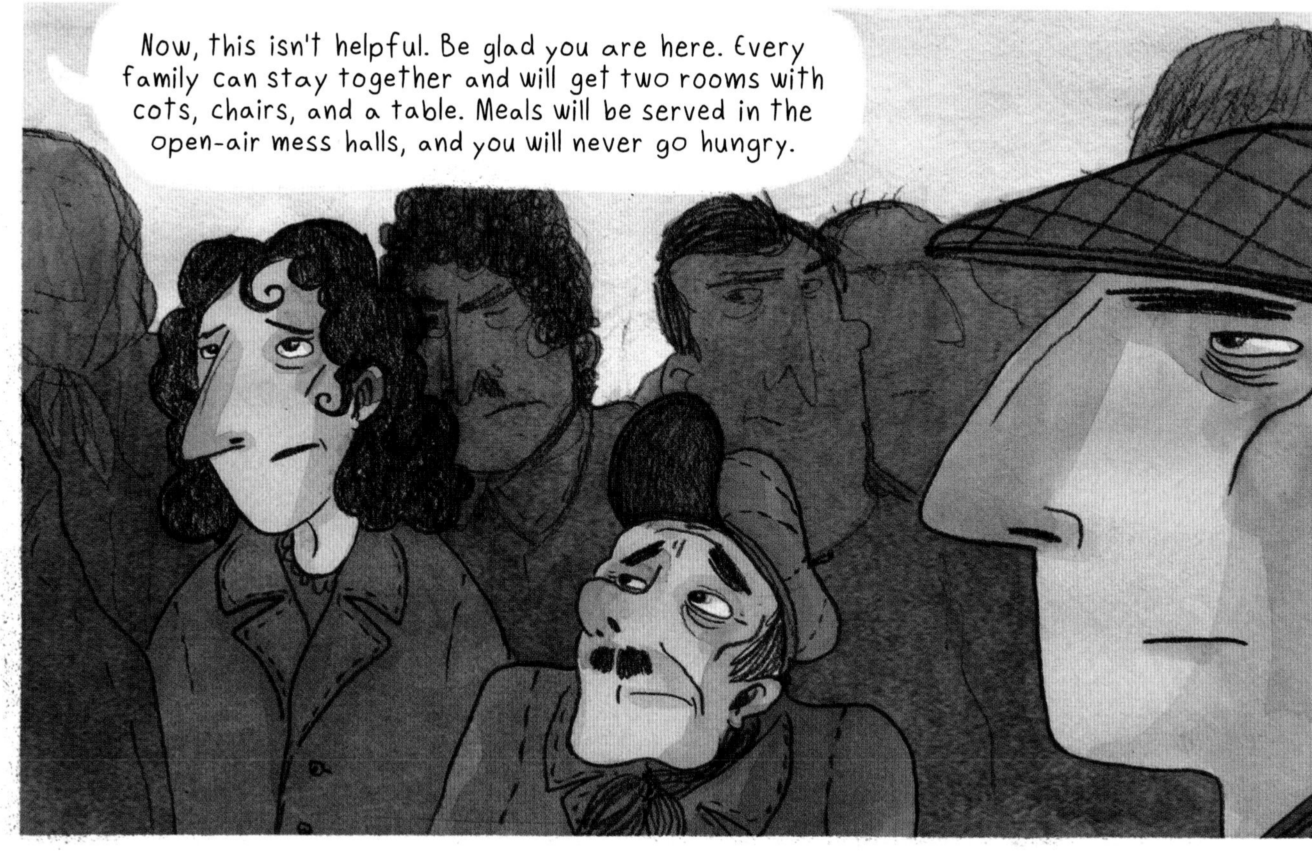
Now, this isn't helpful. Be glad you are here. Every family can stay together and will get two rooms with cots, chairs, and a table. Meals will be served in the open-air mess halls, and you will never go hungry.

If you wish, you may also cook for yourselves. There is a canteen where you can buy supplies. Also recreation halls and a movie theater. I hope that you will have as normal a life as possible while you are here.

But you must follow the rules. First, no one is allowed out of the camp without a pass. Second, nobody is allowed to earn money, to make and sell anything, or to get paid for working.

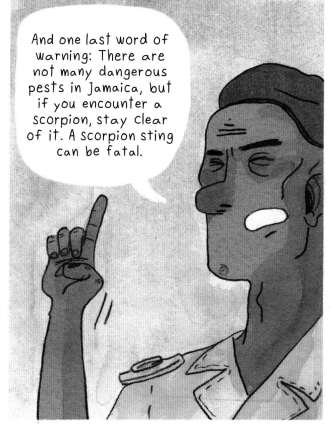

And one last word of warning: There are not many dangerous pests in Jamaica, but if you encounter a scorpion, stay clear of it. A scorpion sting can be fatal.

Scorpions?

31

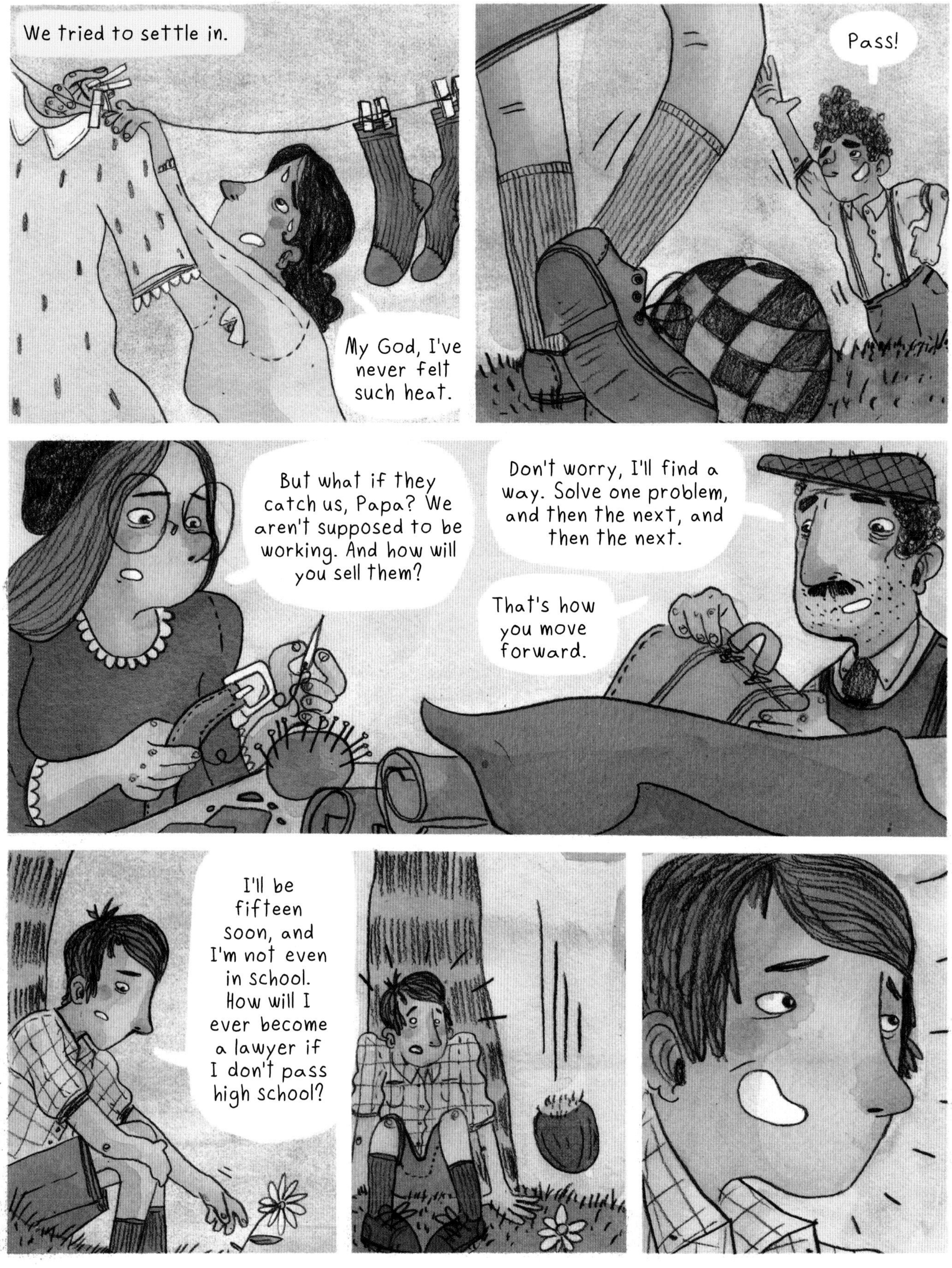
We tried to settle in.
My God, I've never felt such heat.
Pass!
But what if they catch us, Papa? We aren't supposed to be working. And how will you sell them?
Don't worry, I'll find a way. Solve one problem, and then the next, and then the next.
That's how you move forward.
I'll be fifteen soon, and I'm not even in school. How will I ever become a lawyer if I don't pass high school?

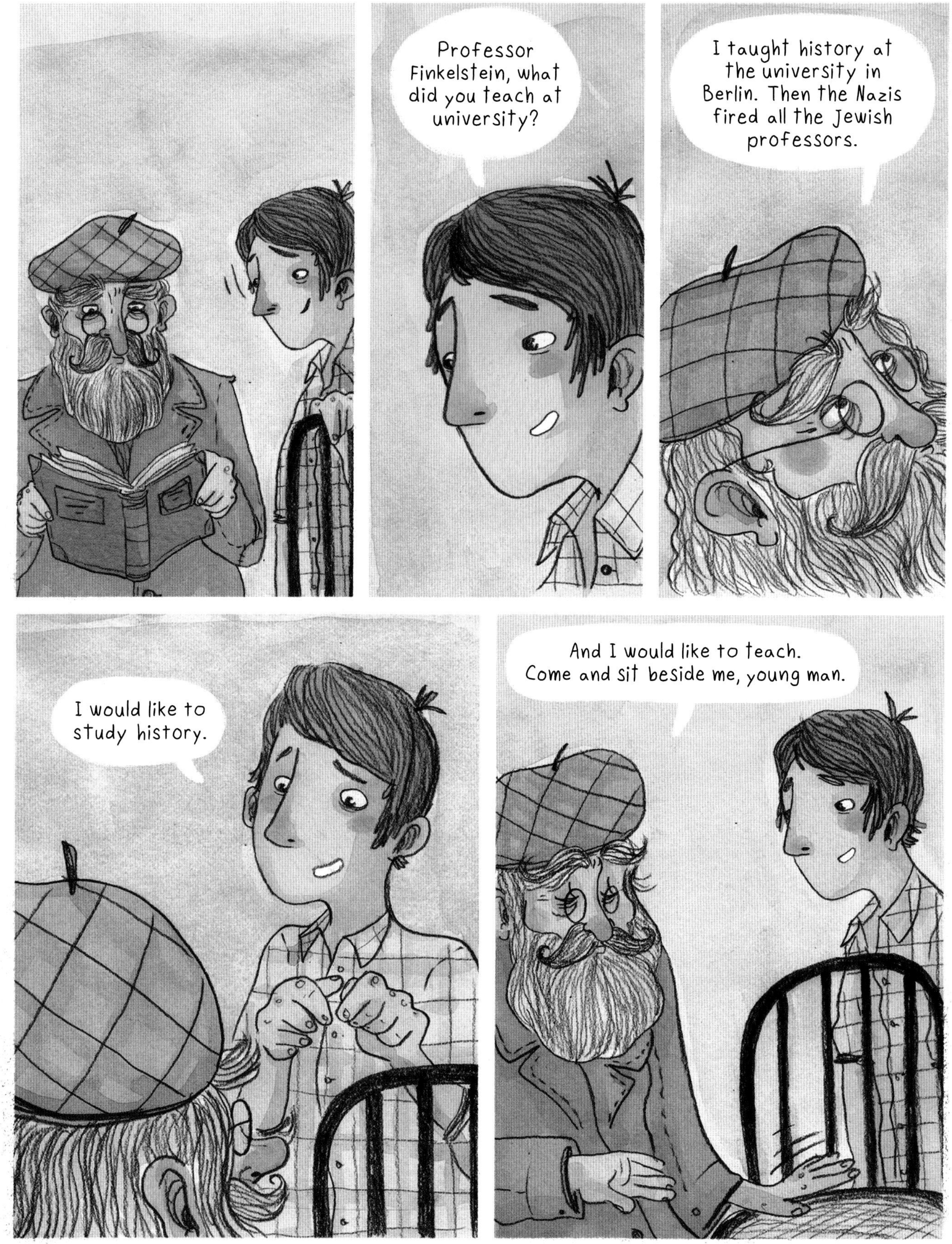

Professor Finkelstein, what did you teach at university?
I taught history at the university in Berlin. Then the Nazis fired all the Jewish professors.
I would like to study history.
And I would like to teach. Come and sit beside me, young man.

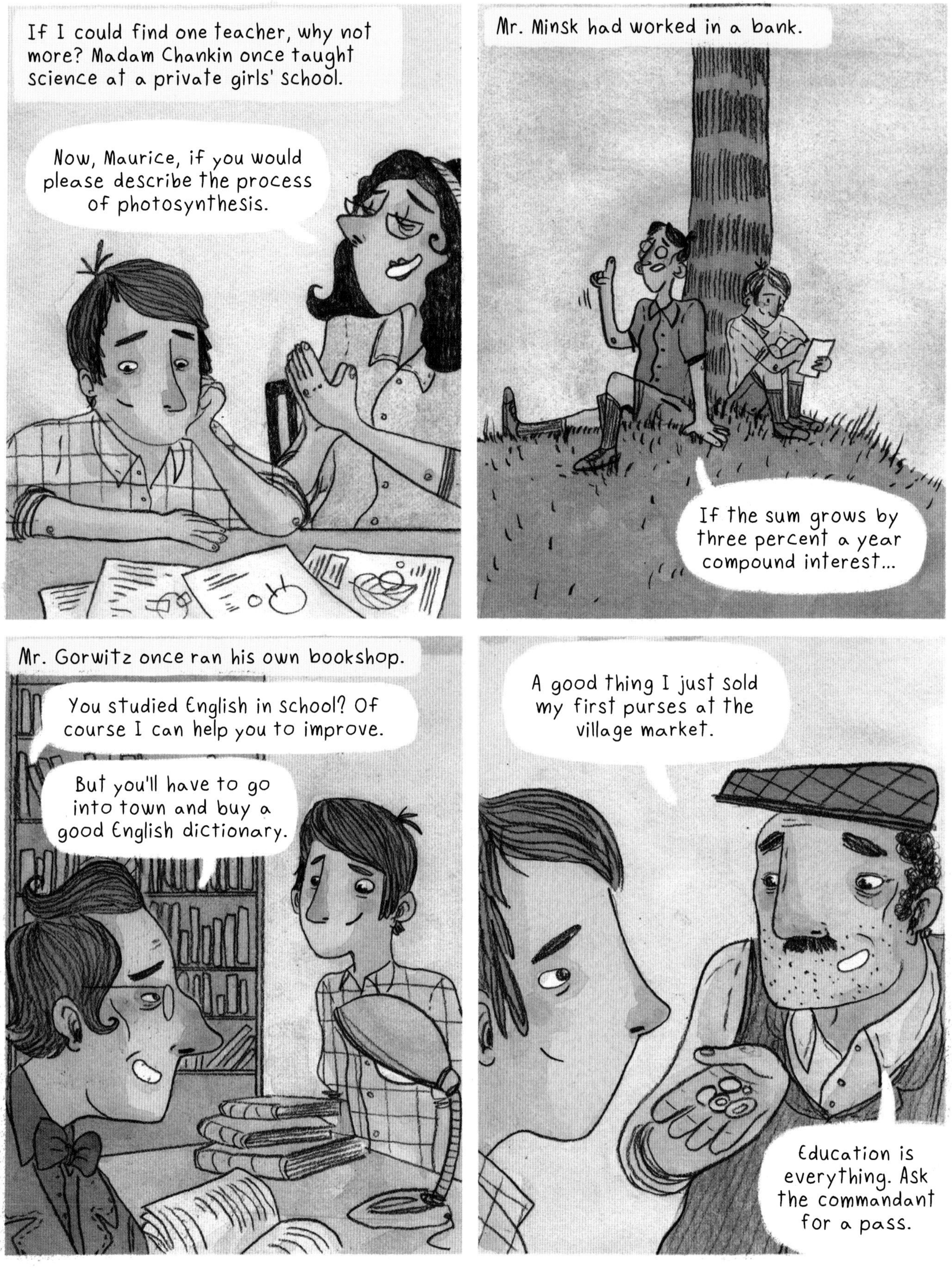
If I could find one teacher, why not more? Madam Chankin once taught science at a private girls' school.
Now, Maurice, if you would please describe the process of photosynthesis.
Mr. Minsk had worked in a bank.
If the sum grows by three percent a year compound interest...
Mr. Gorwitz once ran his own bookshop.
You studied English in school? Of course I can help you to improve.
But you'll have to go into town and buy a good English dictionary.
A good thing I just sold my first purses at the village market.
Education is everything. Ask the commandant for a pass.

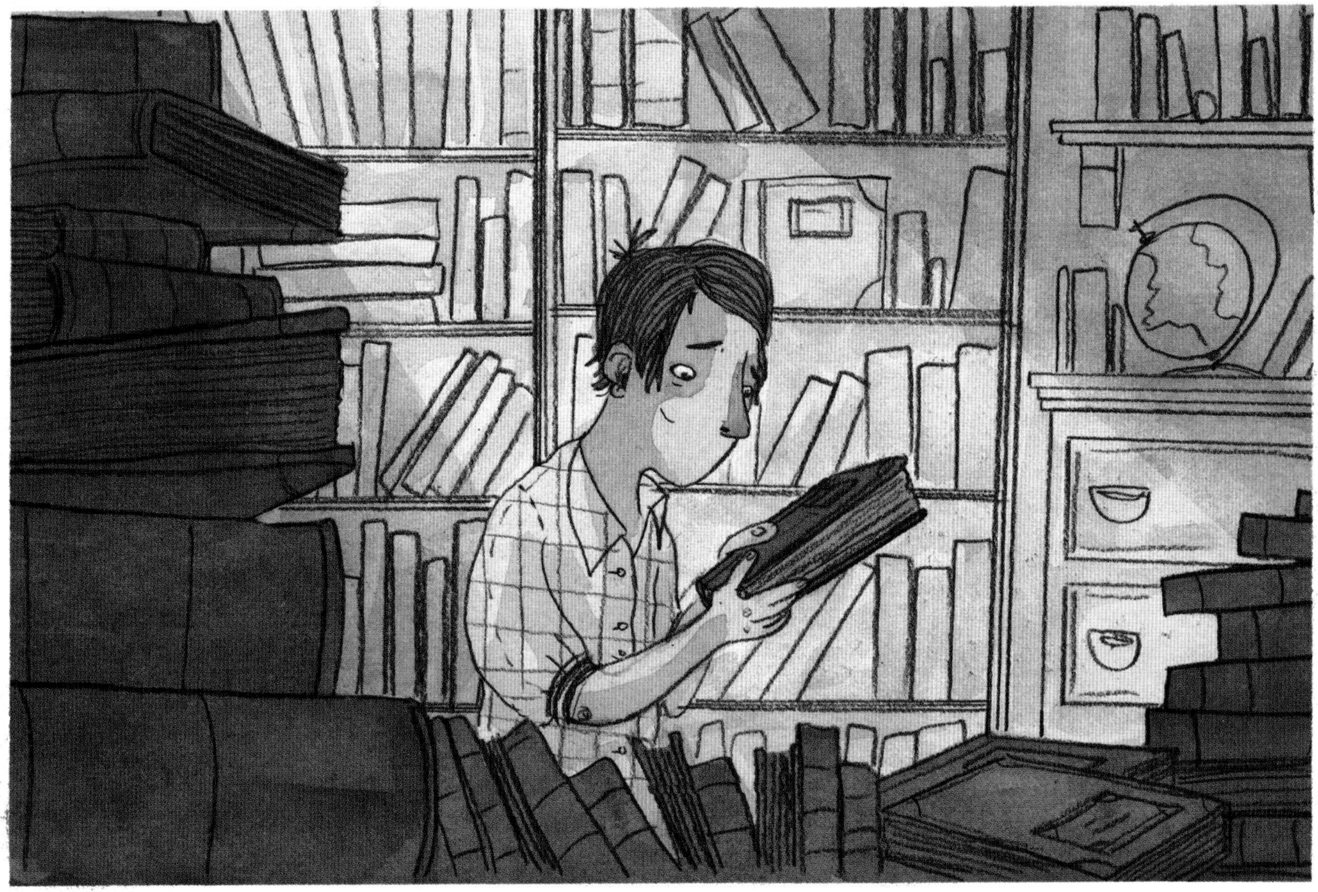

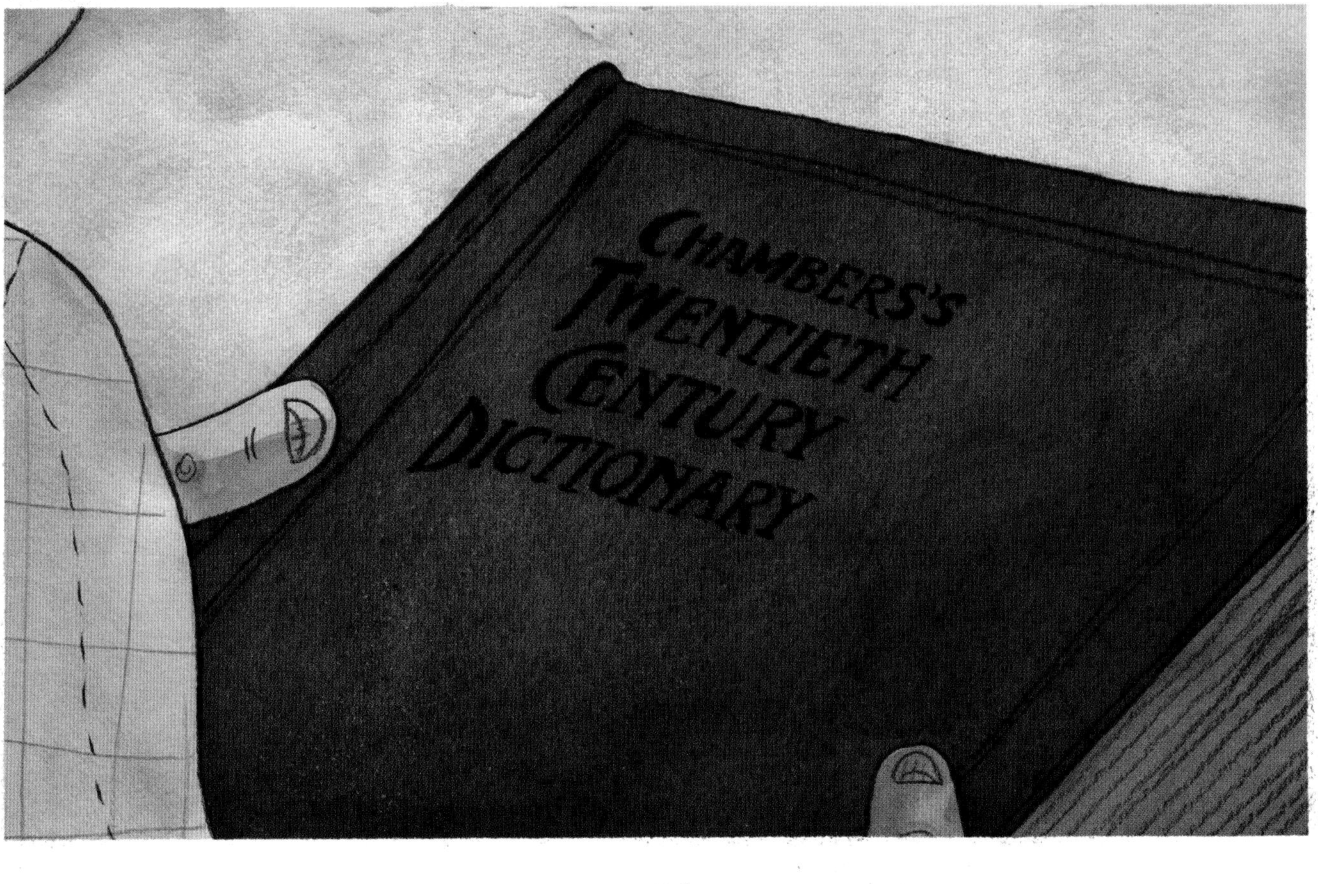
CHAMBERS'S TWENTIETH CENTURY DICTIONARY

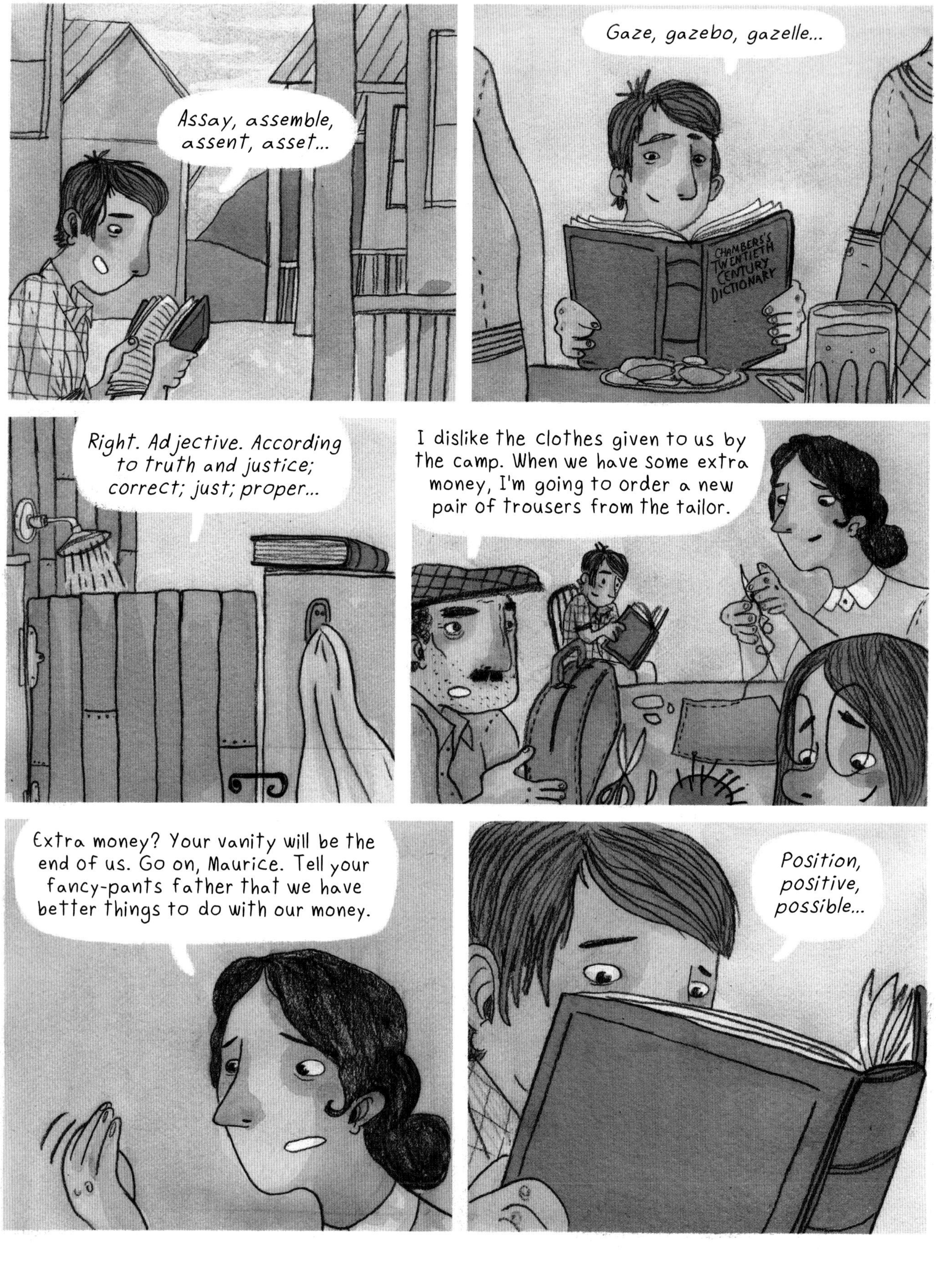
Assay, assemble, assent, asset...
Gaze, gazebo, gazelle...
CHAMBERS'S TWENTIETH CENTURY DICTIONARY
Right. Adjective. According to truth and justice; correct; just; proper...
I dislike the clothes given to us by the camp. When we have some extra money, I'm going to order a new pair of trousers from the tailor.
Extra money? Your vanity will be the end of us. Go on, Maurice. Tell your fancy-pants father that we have better things to do with our money.
Position, positive, possible...

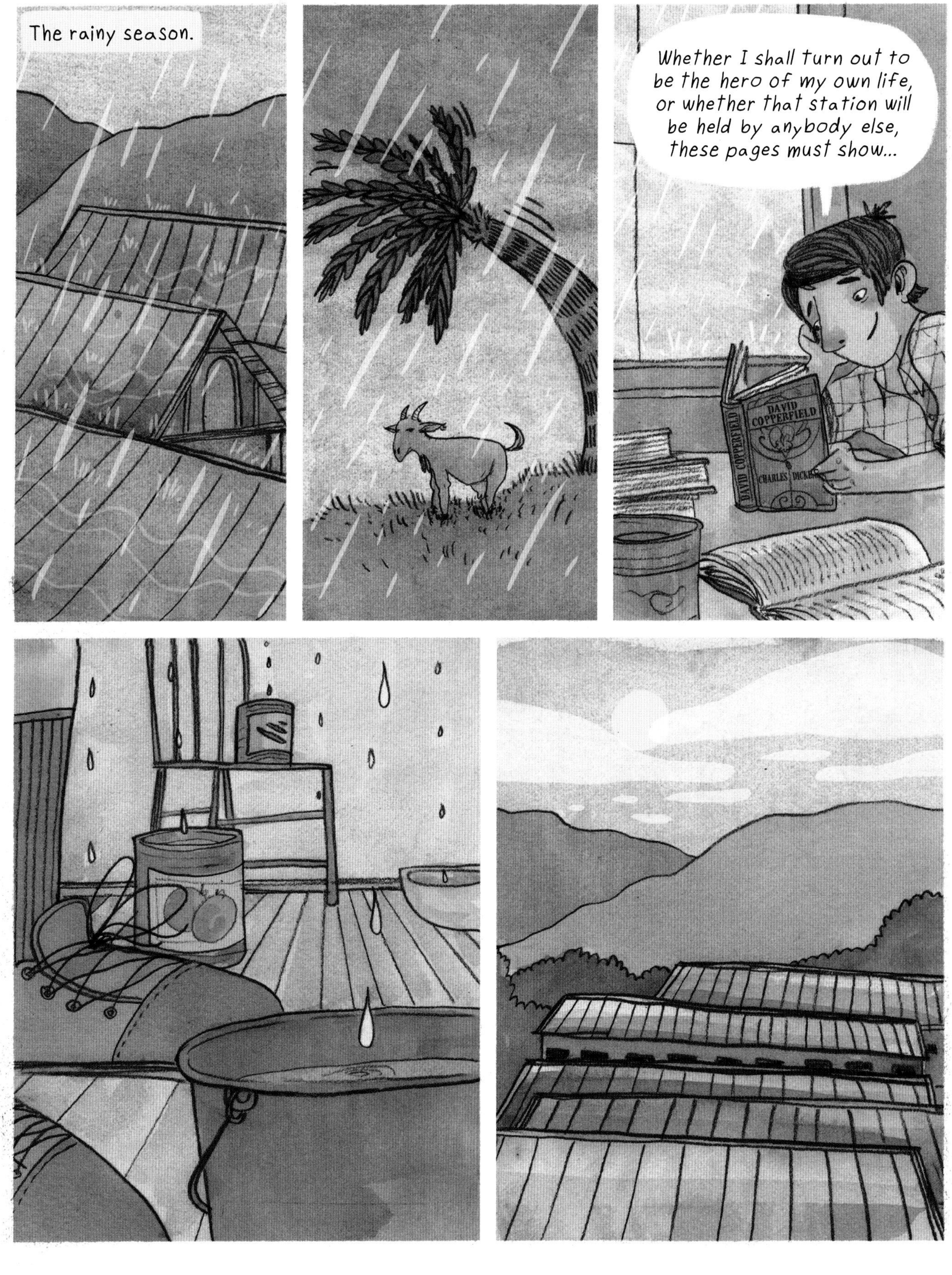
The rainy season.
Whether I shall turn out to be the hero of my own life, or whether that station will be held by anybody else, these pages must show...
DAVID COPPERFIELD
CHARLES DICK

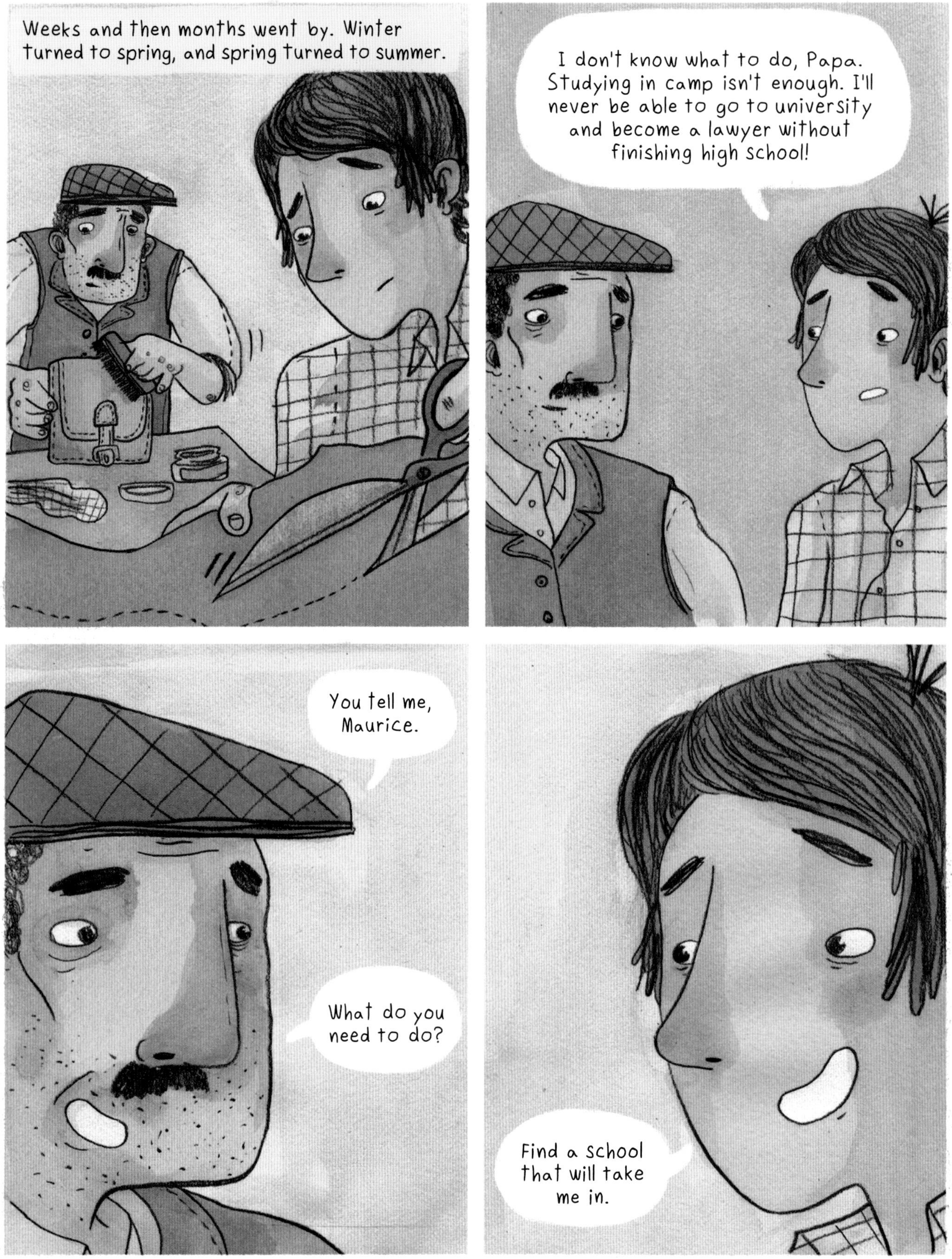
Weeks and then months went by. Winter turned to spring, and spring turned to summer.
I don't know what to do, Papa. Studying in camp isn't enough. I'll never be able to go to university and become a lawyer without finishing high school!
You tell me, Maurice.
What do you need to do?
Find a school that will take me in.

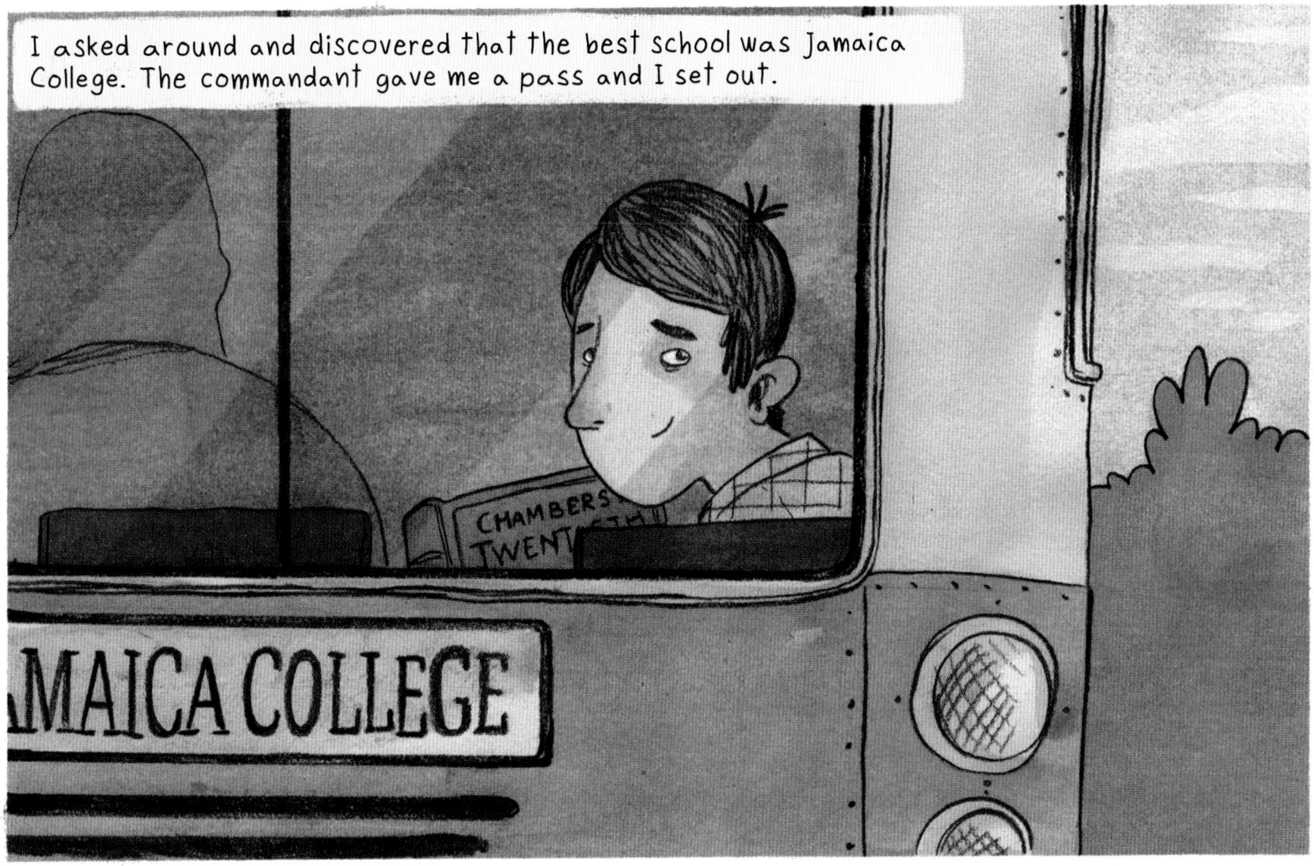
I asked around and discovered that the best school was Jamaica College. The commandant gave me a pass and I set out.
CHAMBERS TWENT
AMAICA COLLEGE

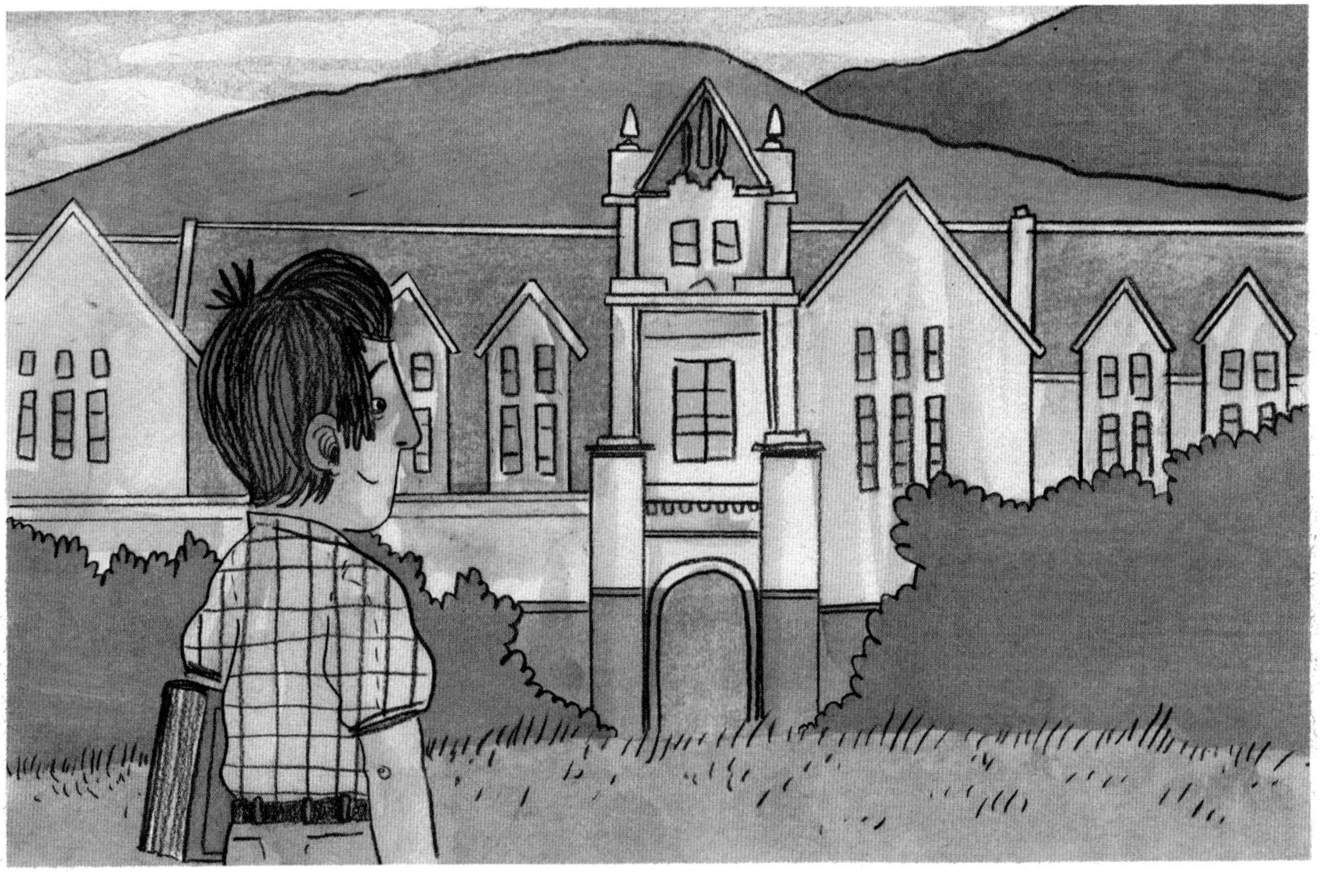

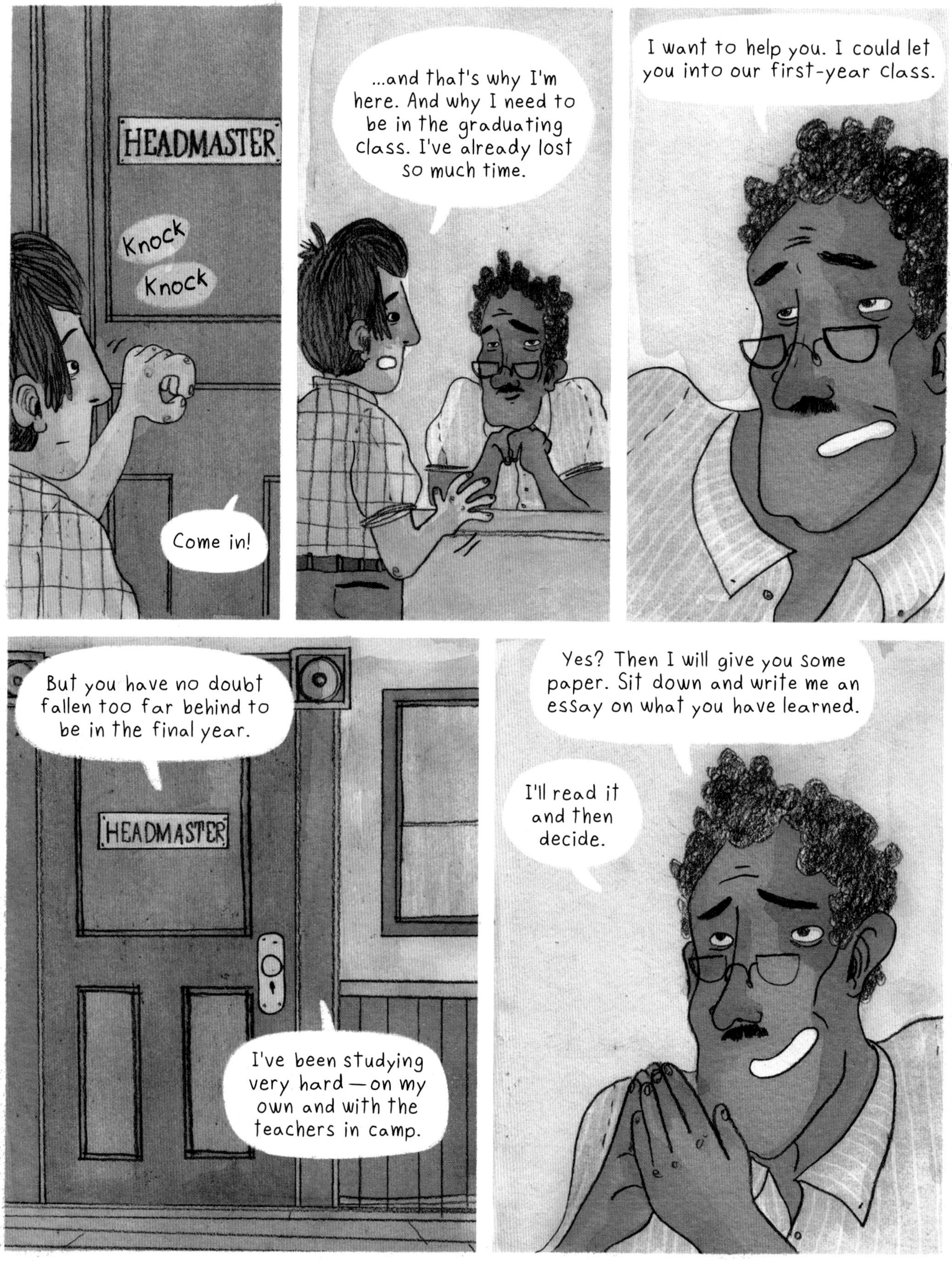
HEADMASTER
Knock
Knock
Come in!
...and that's why I'm here. And why I need to be in the graduating class. I've already lost so much time.
I want to help you. I could let you into our first-year class.
But you have no doubt fallen too far behind to be in the final year.
HEADMASTER
I've been studying very hard — on my own and with the teachers in camp.
Yes? Then I will give you some paper. Sit down and write me an essay on what you have learned.
I'll read it and then decide.

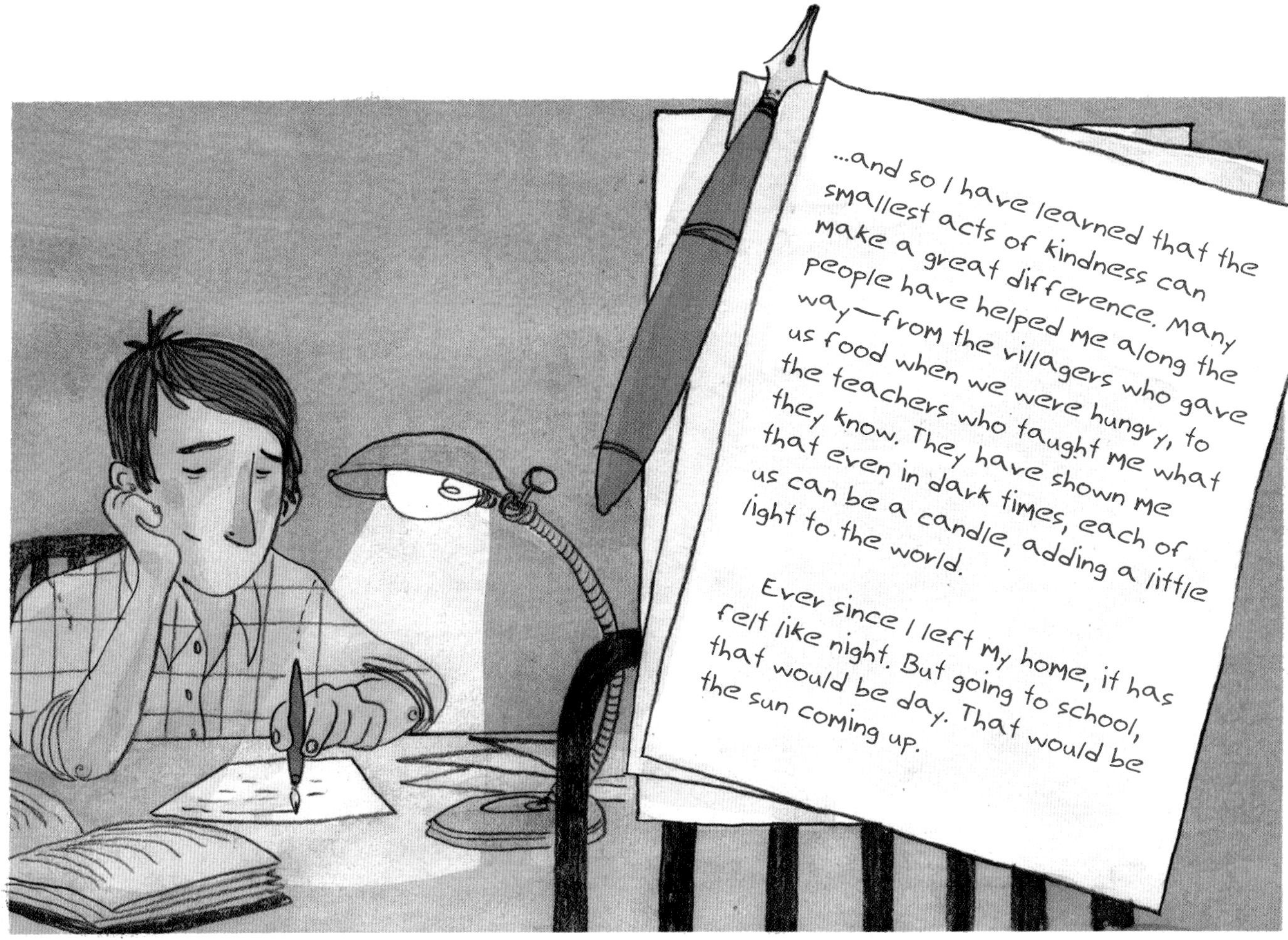
...and so I have learned that the smallest acts of kindness can make a great difference. Many people have helped me along the way—from the villagers who gave us food when we were hungry, to the teachers who taught me what they know. They have shown me that even in dark times, each of us can be a candle, adding a little light to the world.
Ever since I left my home, it has felt like night. But going to school, that would be day. That would be the sun coming up.

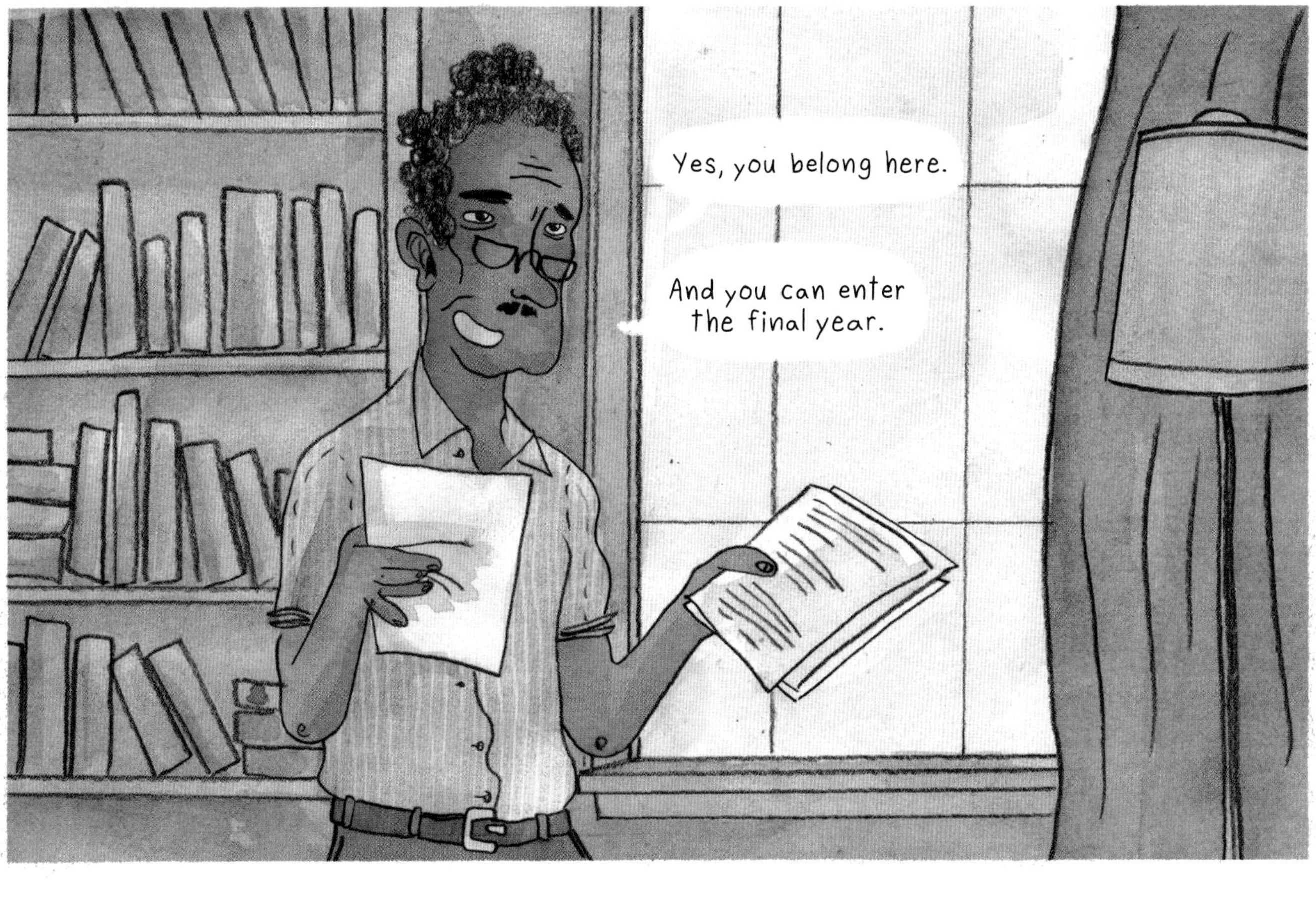
Yes, you belong here.
And you can enter the final year.

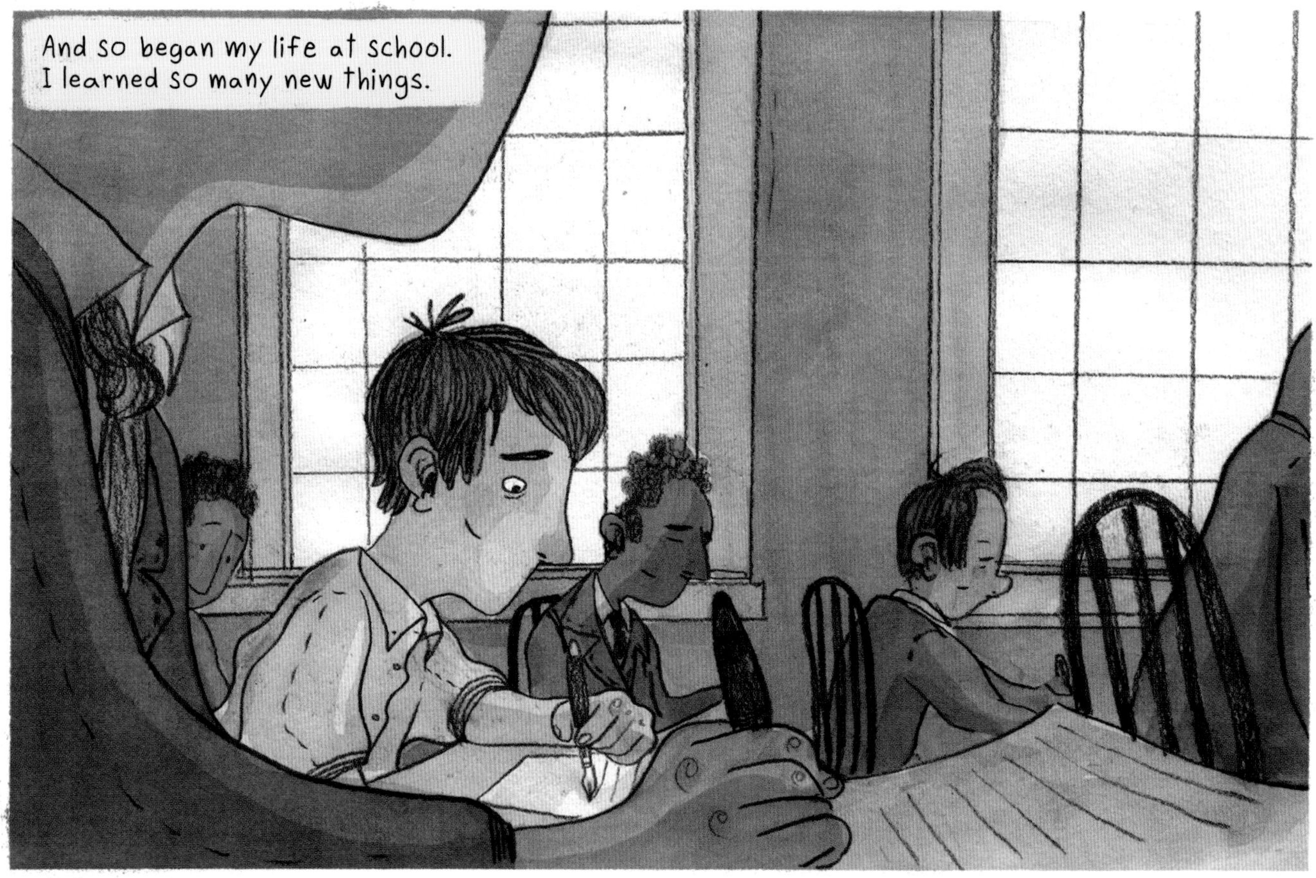
And so began my life at school.
I learned so many new things.

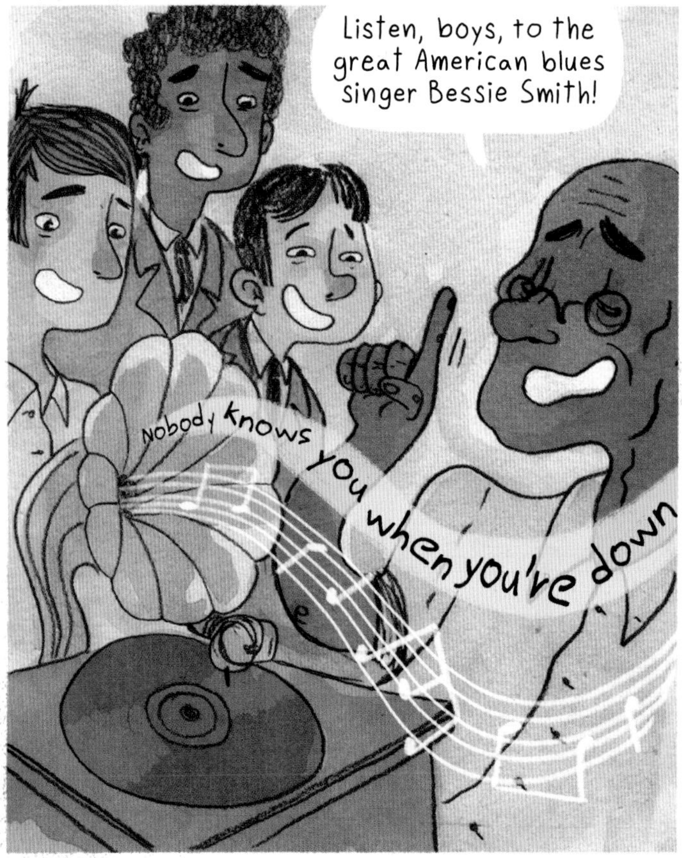
Listen, boys, to the great American blues singer Bessie Smith!
Nobody knows you when you're down

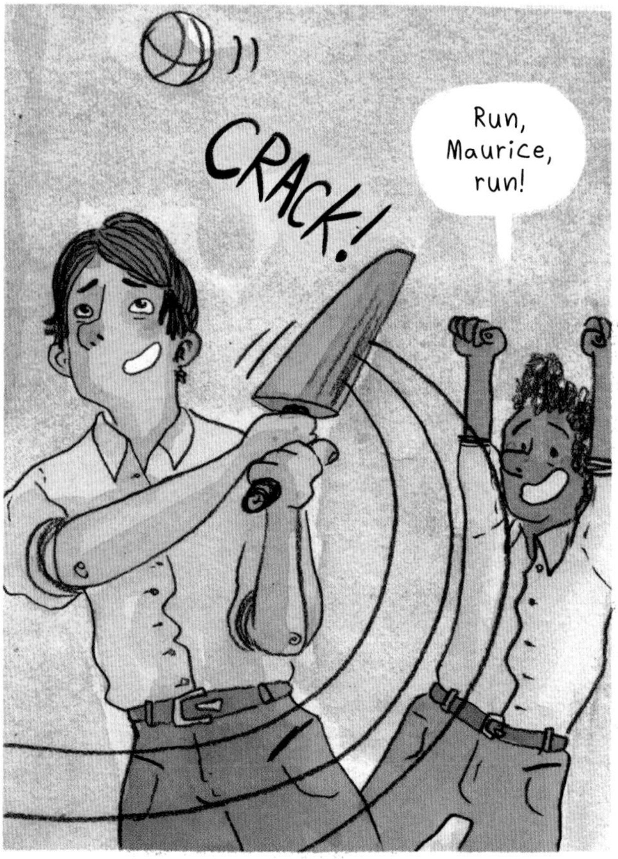
CRACK!
Run, Maurice, run!

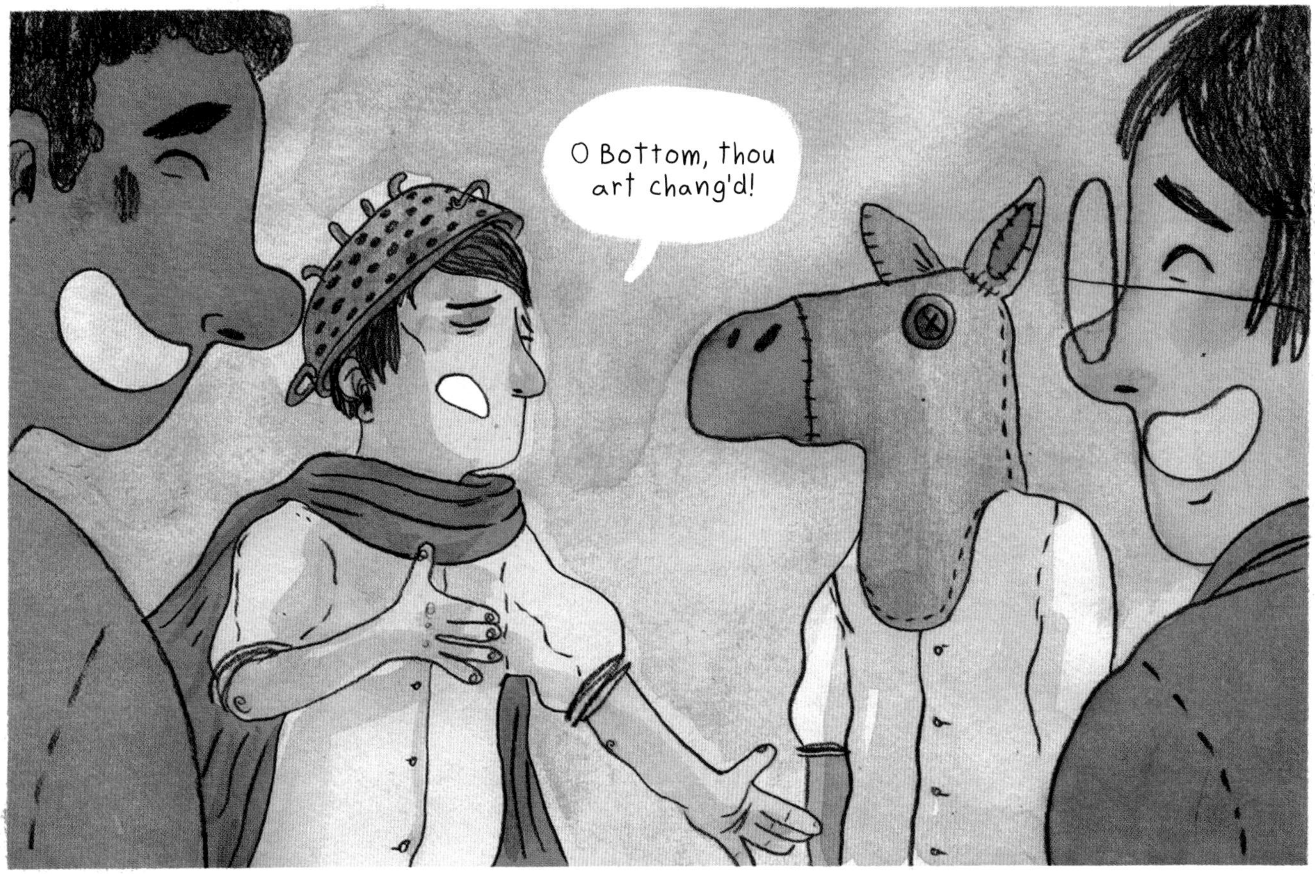
O Bottom, thou art chang'd!

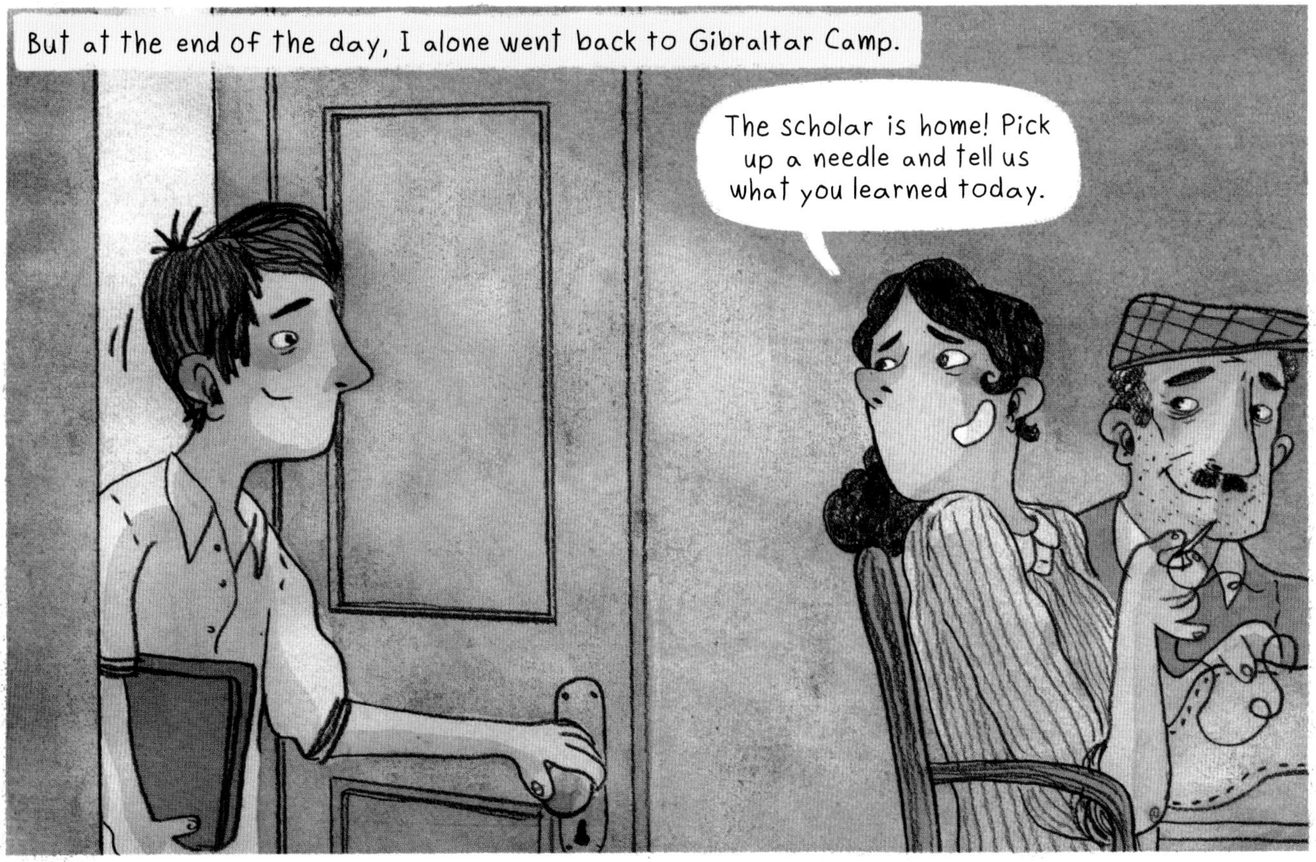
But at the end of the day, I alone went back to Gibraltar Camp.
The scholar is home! Pick up a needle and tell us what you learned today.

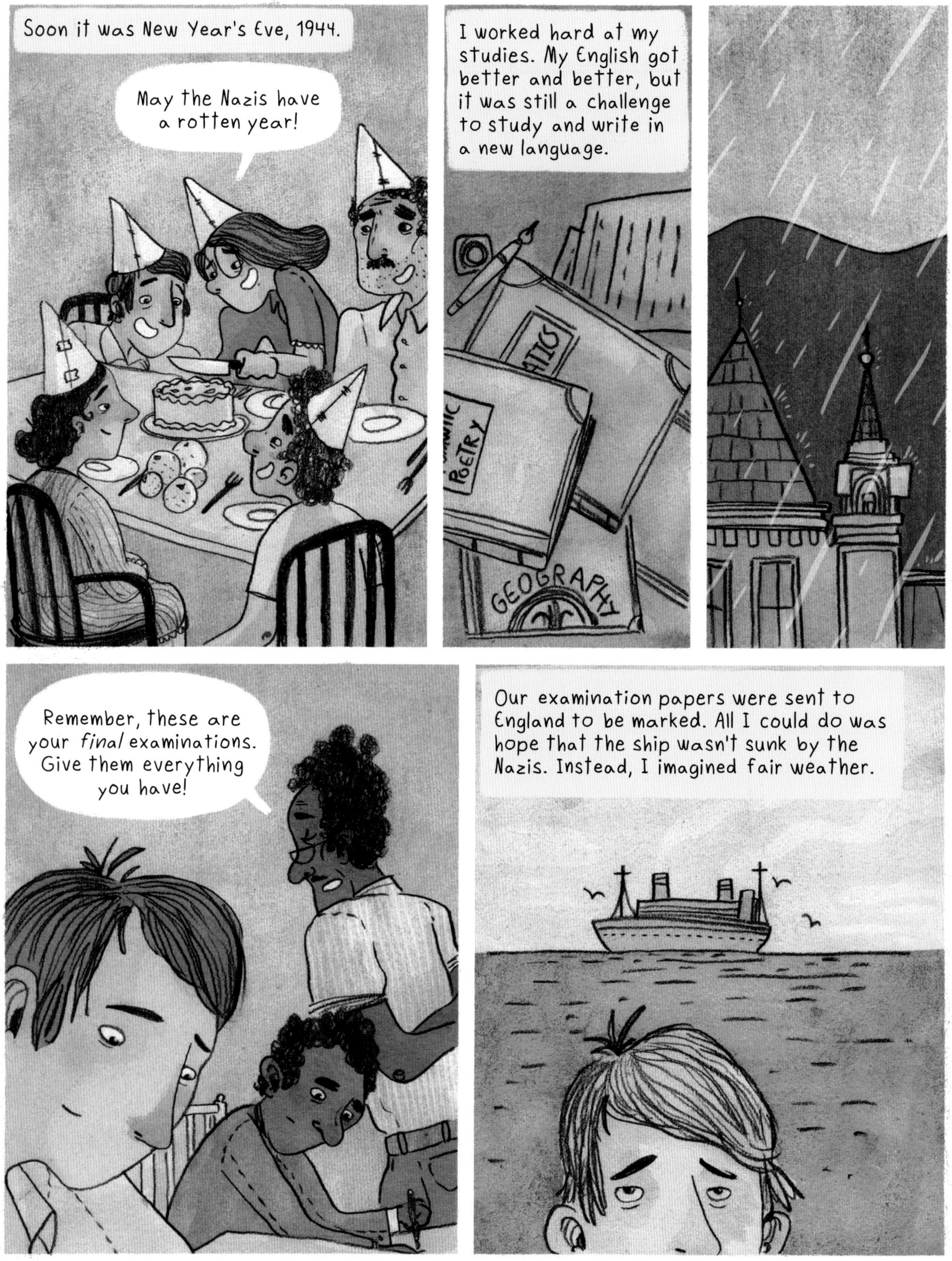
Soon it was New Year's Eve, 1944.
May the Nazis have a rotten year!
I worked hard at my studies. My English got better and better, but it was still a challenge to study and write in a new language.
POETRY
GEOGRAPHY
Remember, these are your *final* examinations. Give them everything you have!
Our examination papers were sent to England to be marked. All I could do was hope that the ship wasn't sunk by the Nazis. Instead, I imagined fair weather.

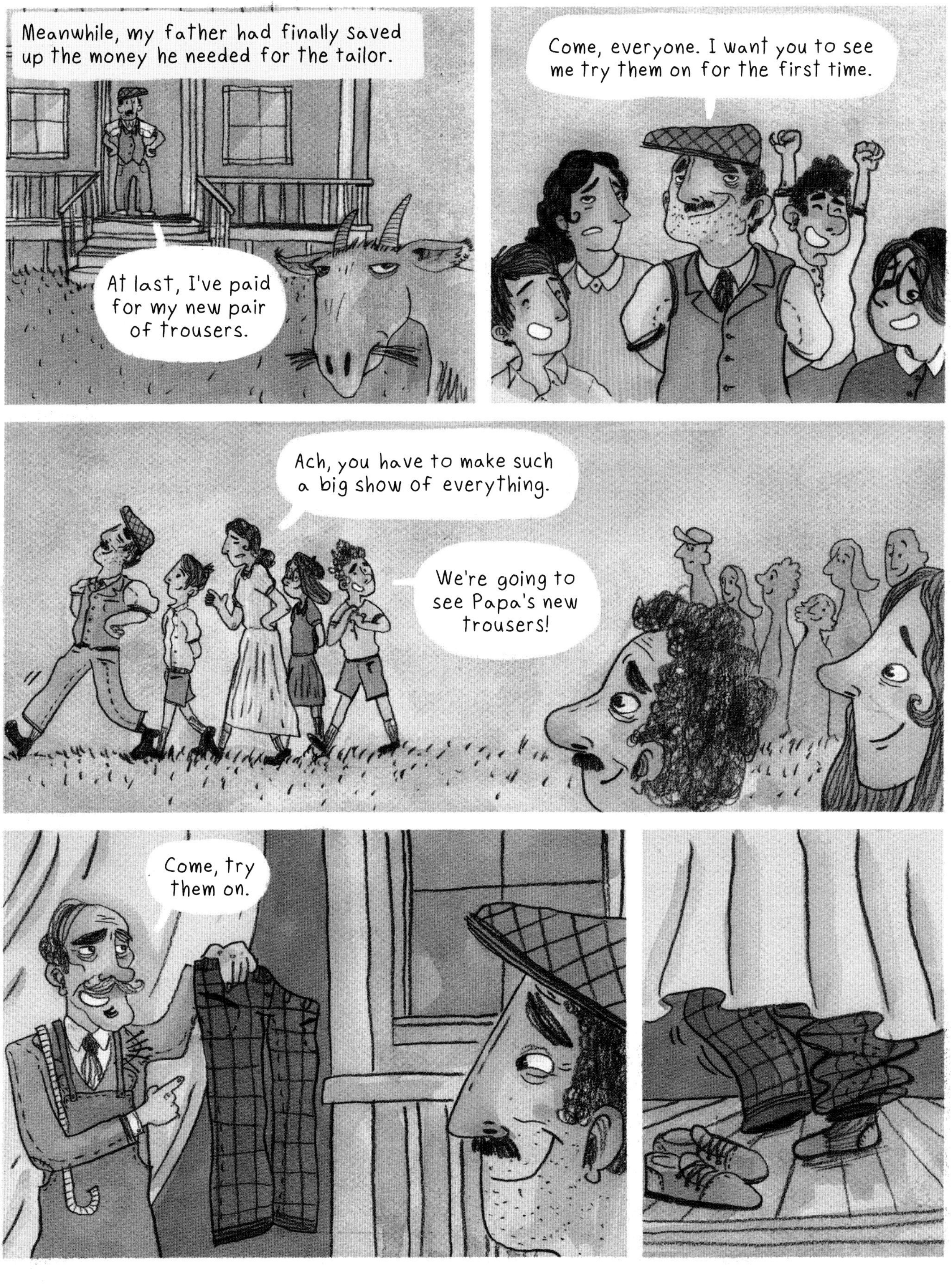
Meanwhile, my father had finally saved up the money he needed for the tailor.
At last, I've paid for my new pair of trousers.
Come, everyone. I want you to see me try them on for the first time.
Ach, you have to make such a big show of everything.
We're going to see Papa's new trousers!
Come, try them on.

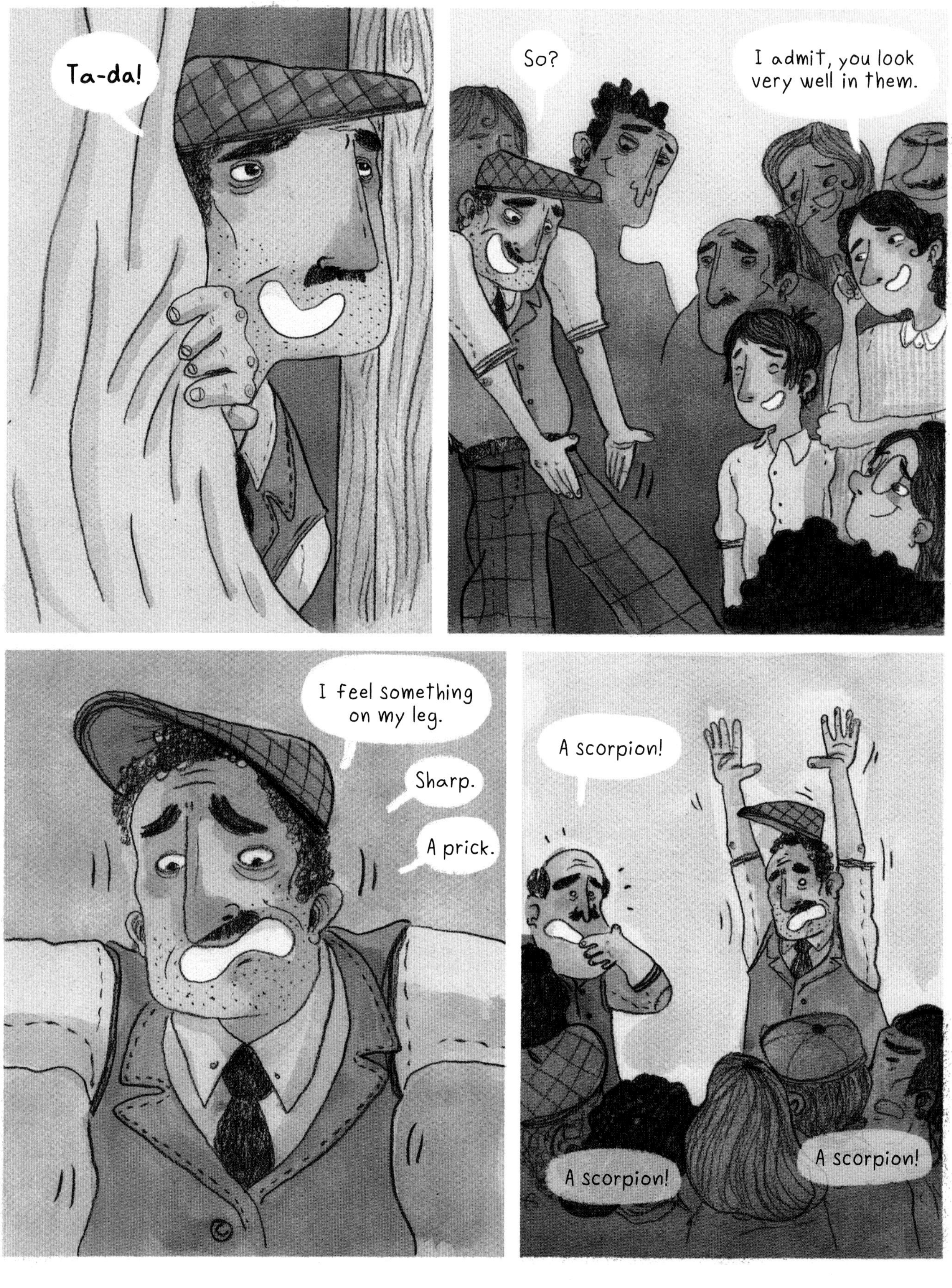
Ta-da!
So?
I admit, you look very well in them.
I feel something on my leg.
Sharp.
A prick.
A scorpion!
A scorpion!
A scorpion!

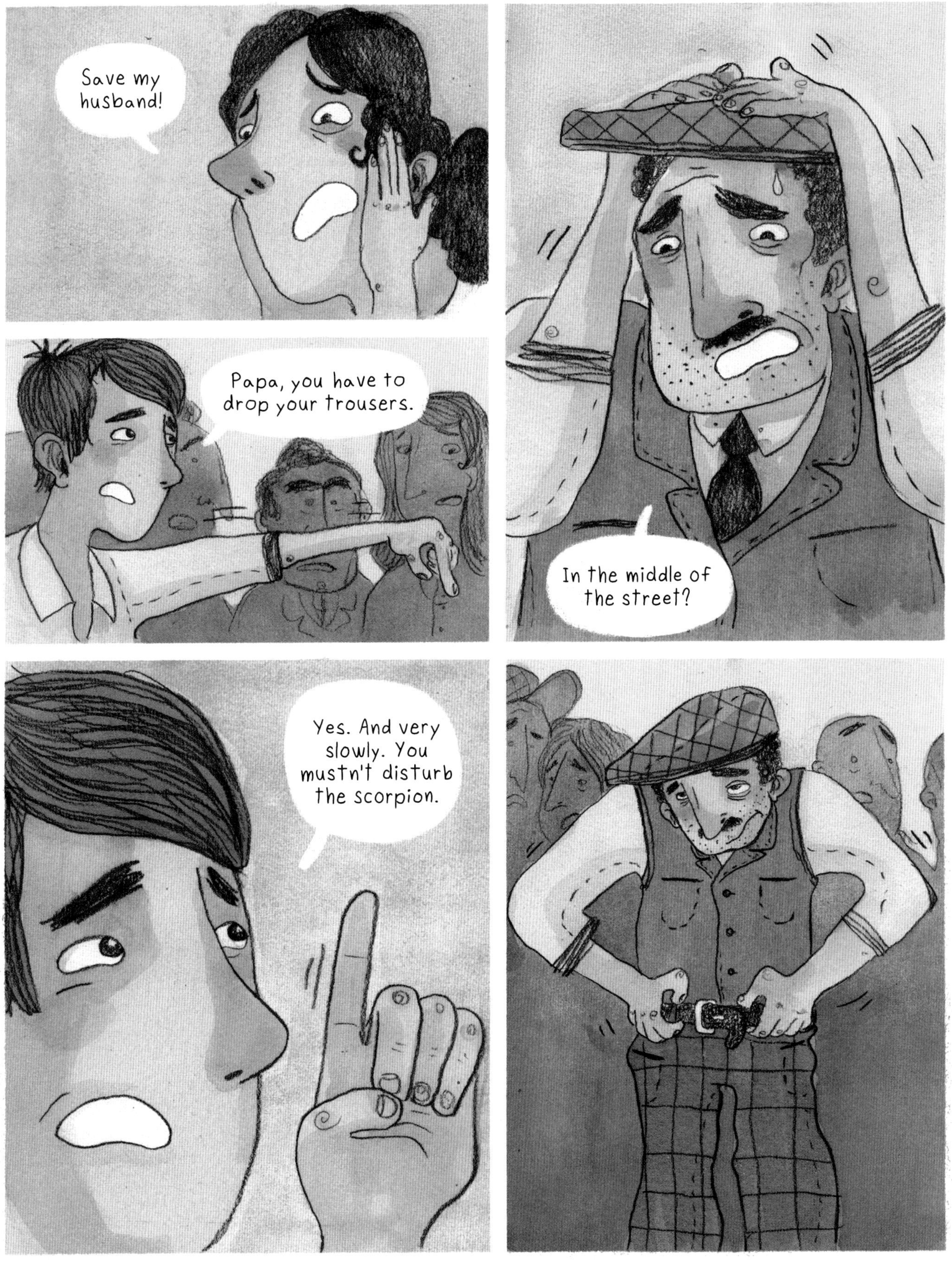
Save my husband!
Papa, you have to drop your trousers.
In the middle of the street?
Yes. And very slowly. You mustn't disturb the scorpion.

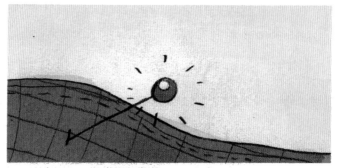

A pin!

I must have left it in by mistake.

Ha ha!

A pin!

VRRRRRRRR

The commandant!

VRRRRRRRRRR

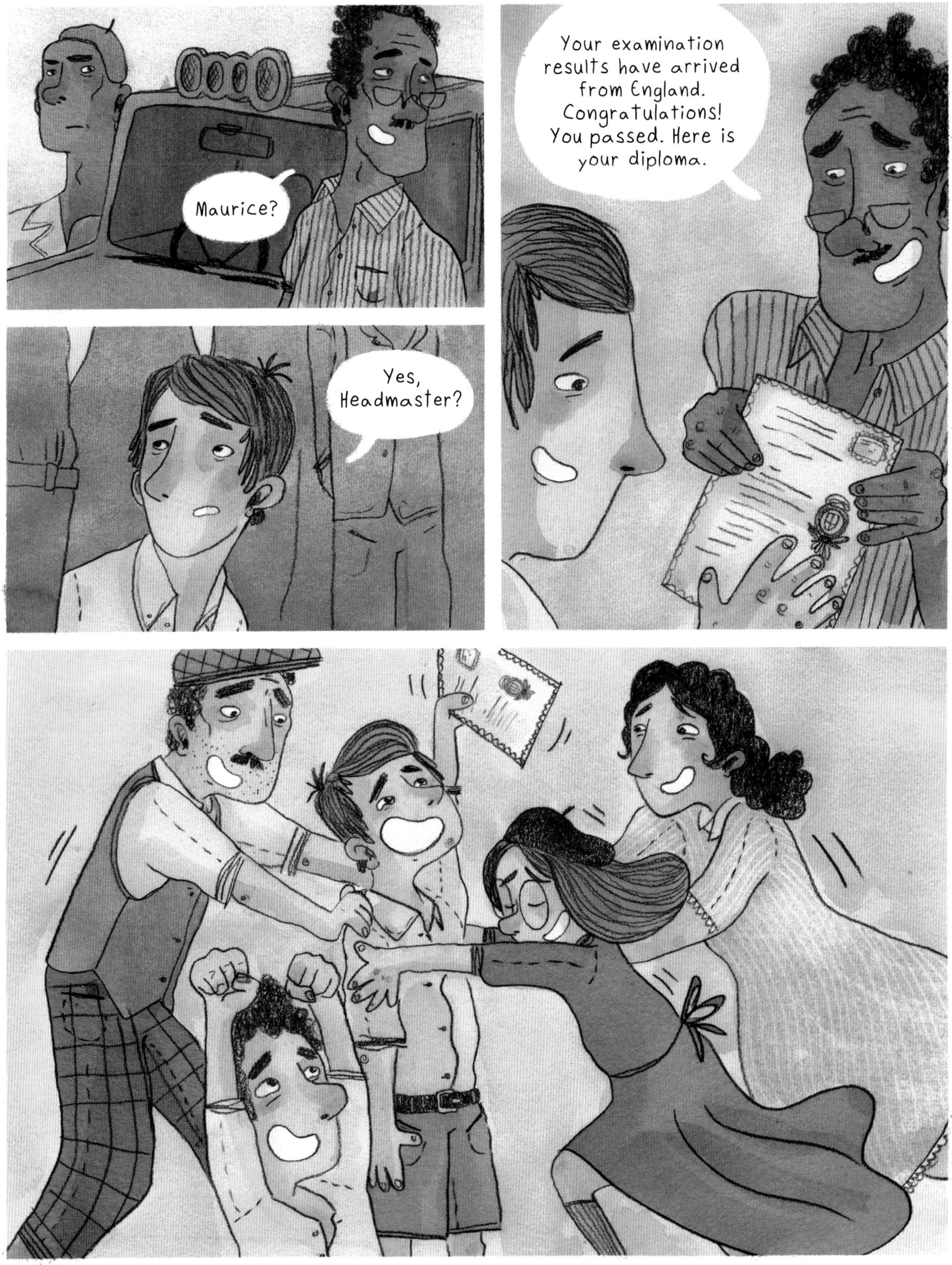
Maurice?
Yes, Headmaster?
Your examination results have arrived from England. Congratulations! You passed. Here is your diploma.

Now that I had my high school diploma, I could apply to universities.

Some of my best instructors have come from the University of Toronto. Canada would be a good place to start a new life.

Several weeks later, a letter arrived. And I learned once more that it wasn't easy to start over.

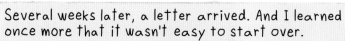

Dear Maurice Fajgenbaum,

We regret to inform you that we cannot accept you at this time. Students must be at least seventeen years old, and you are only sixteen. We would be happy to consider your application again in a year's time.

Sincerely,

D. Rapp, Registrar

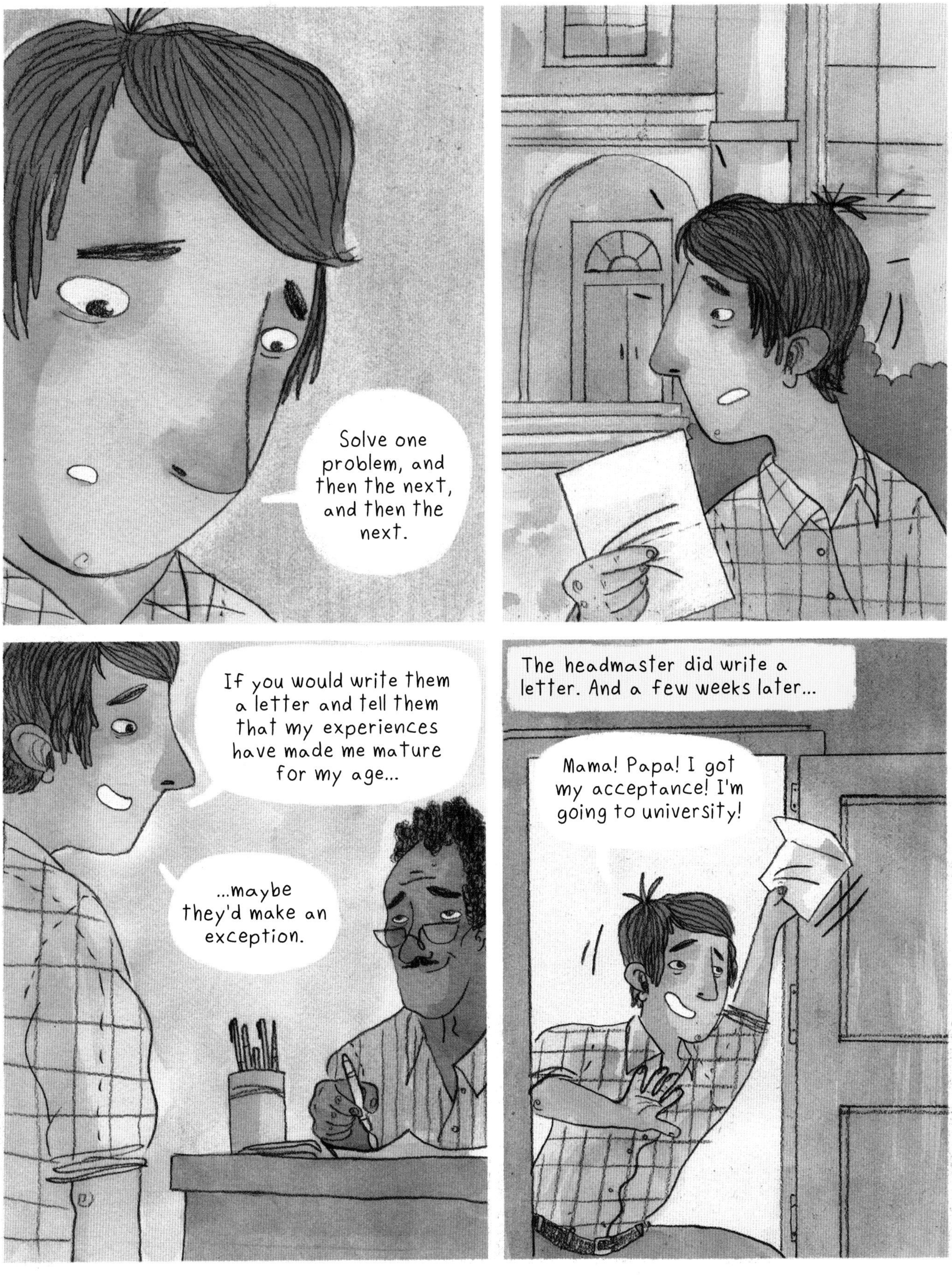
Solve one problem, and then the next, and then the next.
If you would write them a letter and tell them that my experiences have made me mature for my age...
...maybe they'd make an exception.
The headmaster did write a letter. And a few weeks later...
Mama! Papa! I got my acceptance! I'm going to university!

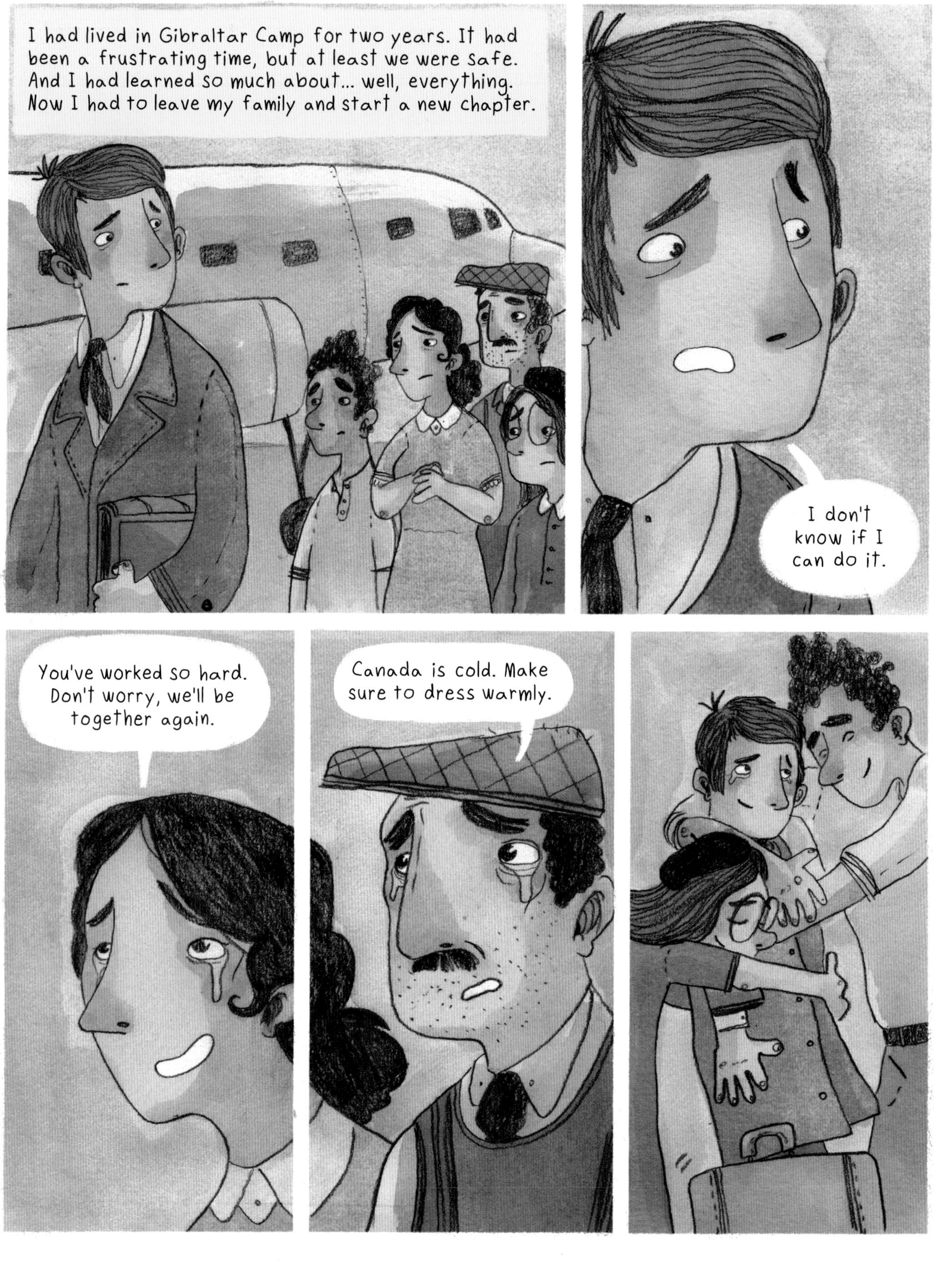
I had lived in Gibraltar Camp for two years. It had been a frustrating time, but at least we were safe. And I had learned so much about... well, everything. Now I had to leave my family and start a new chapter.
I don't know if I can do it.
You've worked so hard. Don't worry, we'll be together again.
Canada is cold. Make sure to dress warmly.

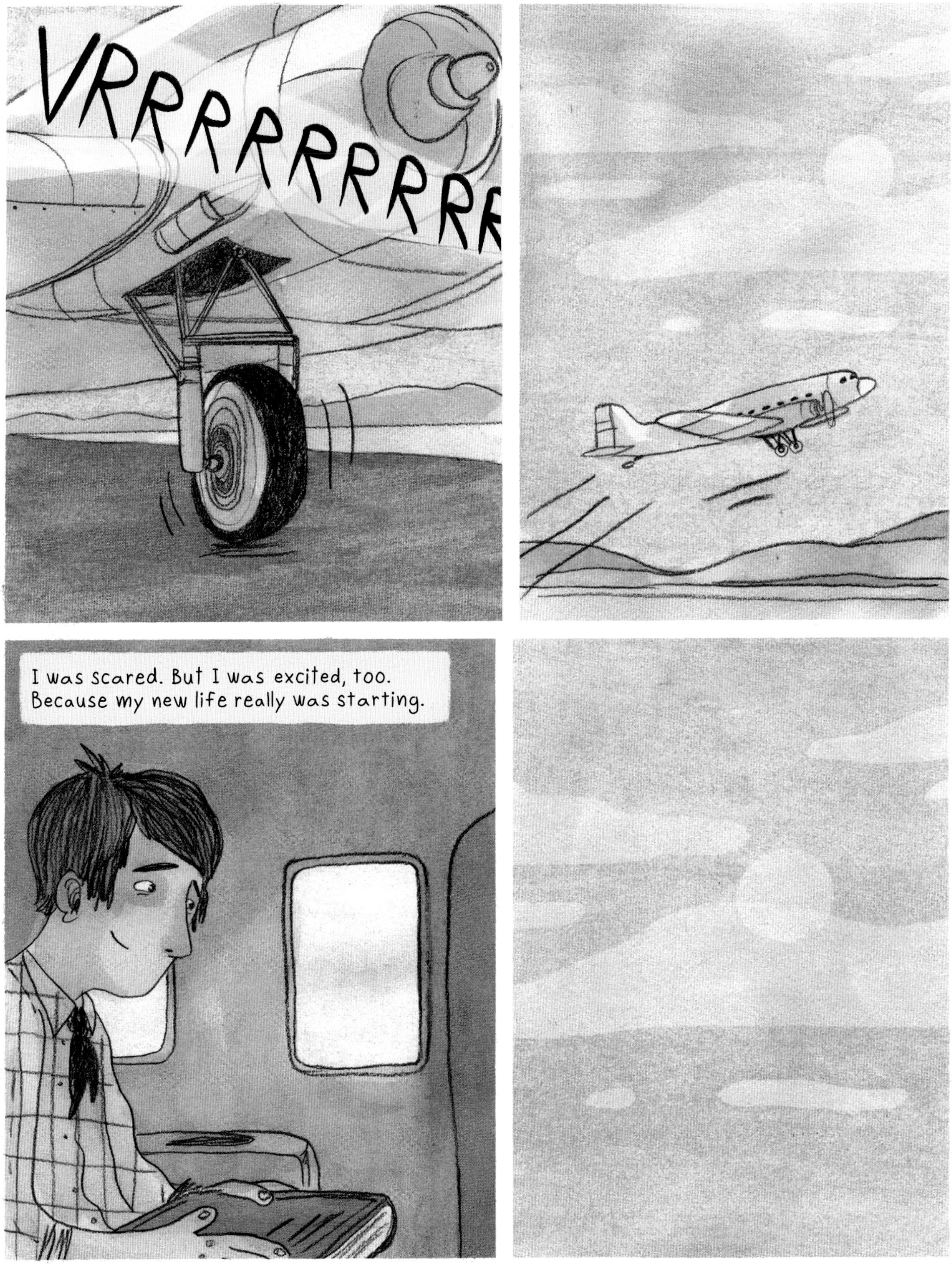
VRRRRRRRRR
I was scared. But I was excited, too.
Because my new life really was starting.

Author's Note

The family, including Maurice's aunt, in front of their home in Brussels. Maurice is at the bottom of the stairs.

Maurice and His Dictionary is based on the life of my father, Maurice; his parents (my grandparents), Adèle and Max; and his older siblings, Adeline and Henri.

My father, Maurice Fajgenbaum, was born in Warsaw, Poland, in 1928. When he was a young child, his family moved to Brussels, Belgium. His first language was French, although at home they also spoke Yiddish (the language of Eastern European Jews). He still had aunts and uncles and cousins living in Poland, and he met them once, on a visit in 1939. All of them perished in the Holocaust.

My father's immediate family was lucky enough to escape. But when he finally arrived in Toronto, Ontario, he did so on a student visa. The Canadian government was at the time refusing to accept Jewish refugees, a shameful period

For their voyage to Jamaica, Maurice's family is listed on the ship's passenger list by their original Polish names.

AMERICAN JOINT DISTRIBUTION COMMITTEE
242 Rua Aurea
Lisbon, Portugal

January 24th, 1942

PASSENGERS SAILED SS SERPA PINTO DESTINATION JAMAICA

No.	N A M E	FIRST NAME	AGE	NO.	N A M E	FIRST NAME	AGE
1.	BERKENBAUM	David	52	34.	ERTAG	Uryas	43
2.	BIEDERMANN	Nathan	31	35.	FAJGENBAUM	Majer	39
				36.		Alta	41
3.	BIELER	Erna	28	37.		Chaje	18
				38.		Hirsch	16
		Chaim	52	39.		Mojsze	14

7

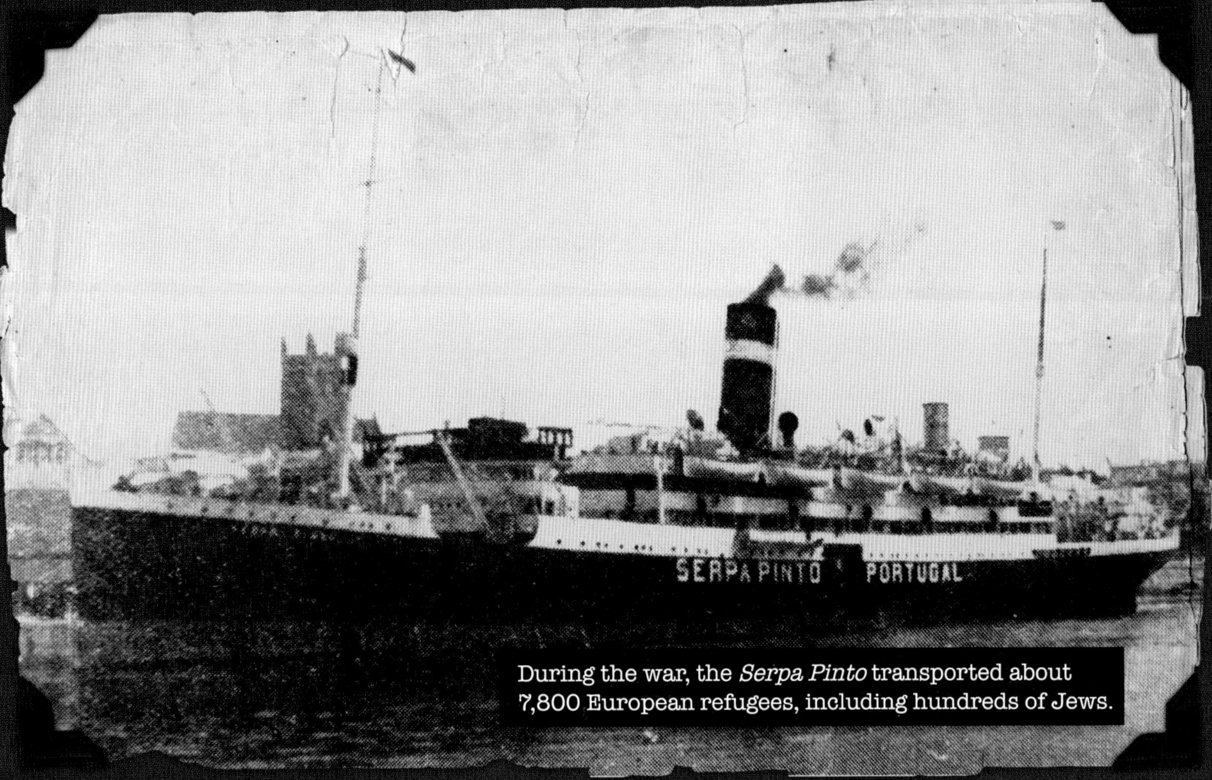
SERPA PINTO PORTUGAL
During the war, the *Serpa Pinto* transported about 7,800 European refugees, including hundreds of Jews.

documented in the book *None Is Too Many: Canada and the Jews of Europe, 1933–1948* by Irving Abella and Harold Troper.

When I was growing up, my father often talked about this time, and eventually he wrote a short memoir for the family, which I've drawn on here. All the important details are as he remembered them, although of course I have made some minor changes. I've also created the scenes and conversations, and I have tried to imagine what my father and his family thought and felt.

Also of great help was *Dreams of Re-Creation in Jamaica: The Holocaust, Internment, Jewish Refugees in Gibraltar Camp, Jamaican Jews and Sephardim* by Diana Cooper-Clark. Professor Cooper-Clark's excellent book provided useful details and dates, and captures well what life was like in Gibraltar Camp. Among the people she interviewed was my father.

In Toronto, Dad lived in a boarding house, worked at several jobs, attended university, and met my mother. He changed his last name to Fagan.

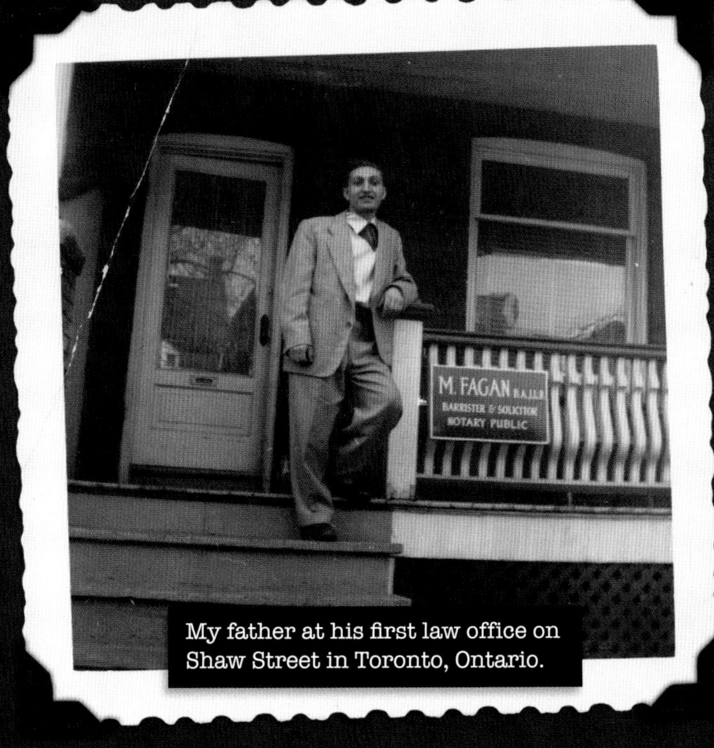
M. FAGAN
BARRISTER & SOLICITOR
NOTARY PUBLIC
My father at his first law office on Shaw Street in Toronto, Ontario.

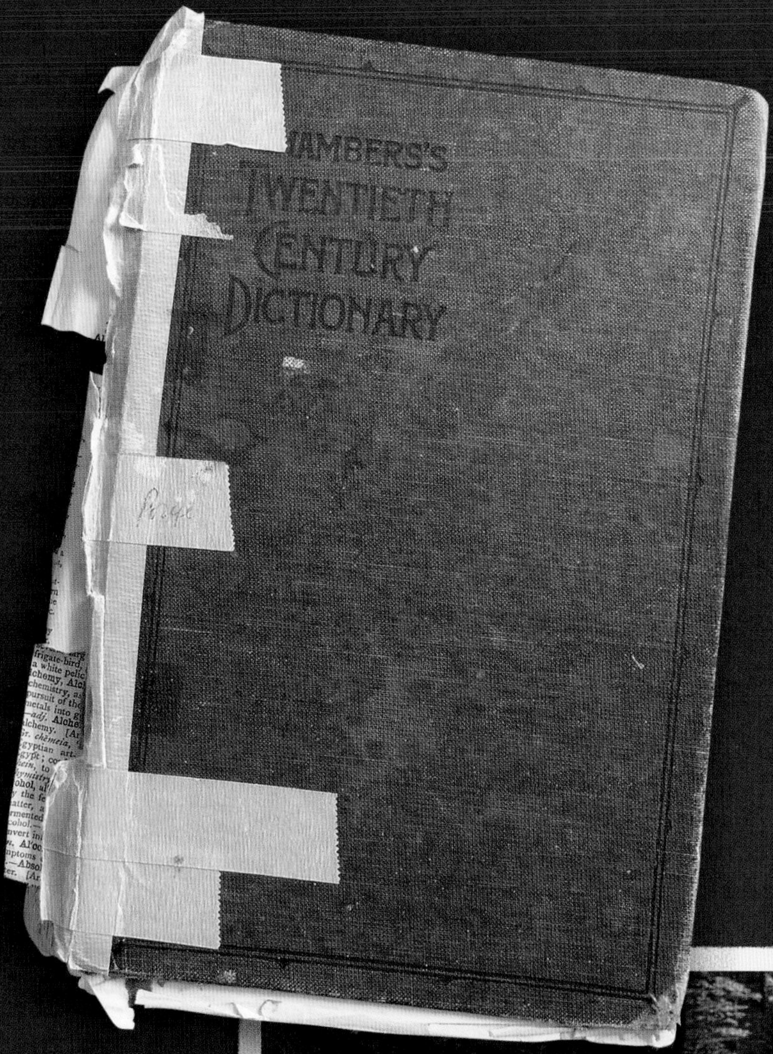
CHAMBERS'S
TWENTIETH
CENTURY
DICTIONARY

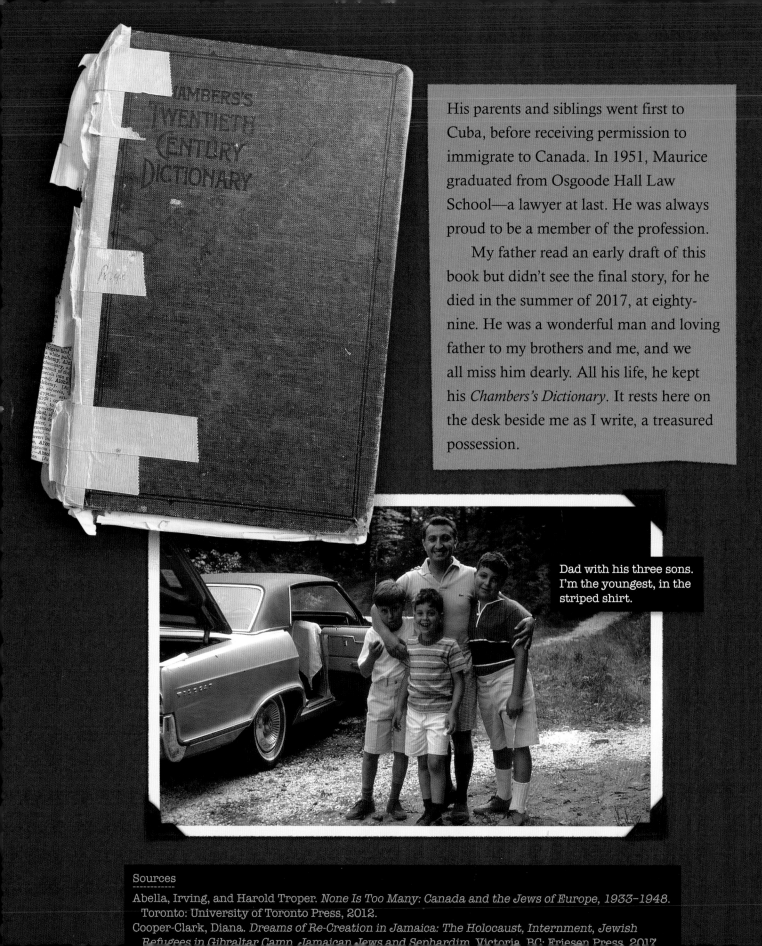

His parents and siblings went first to Cuba, before receiving permission to immigrate to Canada. In 1951, Maurice graduated from Osgoode Hall Law School—a lawyer at last. He was always proud to be a member of the profession.

My father read an early draft of this book but didn't see the final story, for he died in the summer of 2017, at eighty-nine. He was a wonderful man and loving father to my brothers and me, and we all miss him dearly. All his life, he kept his *Chambers's Dictionary*. It rests here on the desk beside me as I write, a treasured possession.

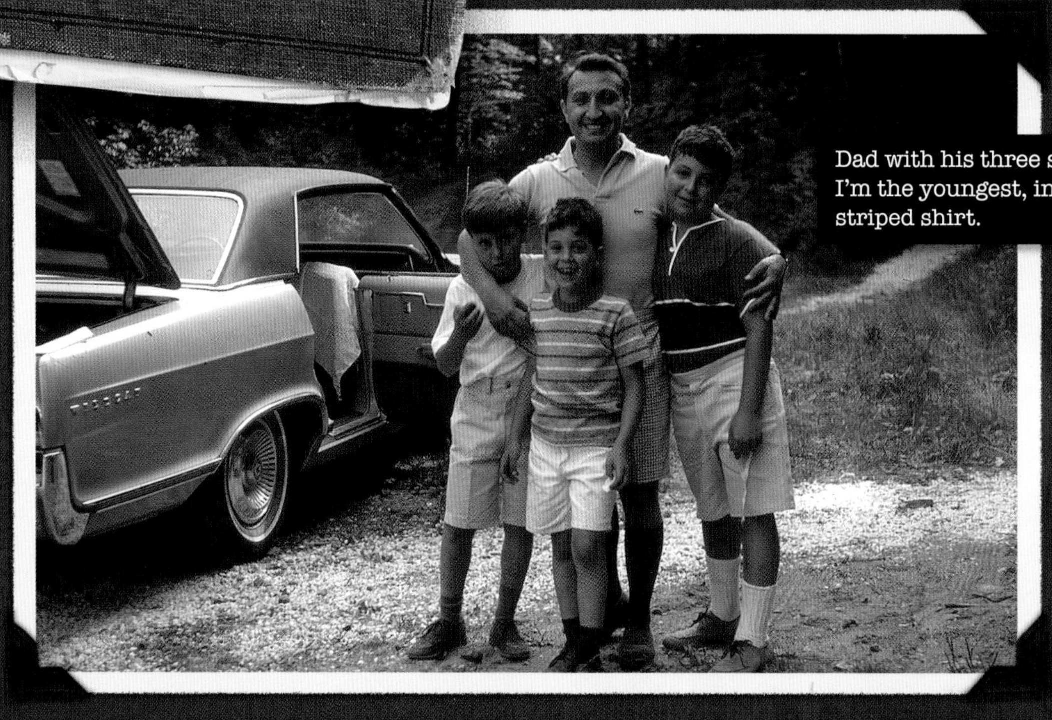

Dad with his three sons. I'm the youngest, in the striped shirt.

Sources

Abella, Irving, and Harold Troper. *None Is Too Many: Canada and the Jews of Europe, 1933–1948.* Toronto: University of Toronto Press, 2012.

Cooper-Clark, Diana. *Dreams of Re-Creation in Jamaica: The Holocaust, Internment, Jewish Refugees in Gibraltar Camp, Jamaican Jews and Sephardim.* Victoria, BC: Friesen Press, 2017.